PRAISE FOR
CAROLINE B. COONEY

PRAISE FOR *THE WRONG GOOD DEED*

"Grit and courage wrapped in charm."

—Sulari Gentill, *USA Today* bestselling author of
The Woman in the Library

PRAISE FOR *BEFORE SHE WAS HELEN*

"[M]ore Columbo than Miss Marple... A fine mystery."

—*Booklist*

"Caroline B. Cooney is a master of taking a small, common moment—seeing a face on a milk carton, posting a harmless photo—and turning that moment into a thrilling story. In this mystery, Cooney gives us Clemmie, a senior citizen living a long deception, who fights back with intelligence and courage against dangerous foes, both present and past. *Before She Was Helen* is an emotionally rich page-turner about the lives we want—and the lives we make."

—Jeff Abbott, *New York Times* bestselling author of *Never Ask Me*

"As *Before She Was Helen* opens, readers are drawn into what appears to be a light, retirement-community caper. But author Caroline B.

Cooney quickly flips expectations upside down in this deceptively dark mystery. Between old crimes and fresh murders, septuagenarian protagonist Clemmie faces an unspeakable fear that will keep readers hooked in this twisty whodunit."

—Julie Hyzy, *New York Times* bestselling author

"Caroline B. Cooney has a genius for skewering culture, crime, and society. As once she demonstrated to the world a pressing level of danger we needed to understand, now she whips millennial angst, recreational drug use, and one feisty, heroic retiree into a thrilling, toxic brew that will leave readers cheering by the end. Retirement villages never seemed so mysterious and exciting! Under Cooney's deft hand, hidden dangers emerge, and the ties that bind us, young and old, just may save us in the end."

—Jenny Milchman, *USA Today* bestselling author of
Cover of Snow and *Wicked River*

"Caroline B. Cooney's *Before She Was Helen* is a clever whodunit featuring an immensely likable septuagenarian heroine with a tragic past. Cooney is deft at weaving together the mysteries of a fifty-year-old cold case murder and a still-warm body at a retirement community, slowly unveiling a slew of possible motives and suspects for both crimes. Loaded with action, fast-paced, and offering a series of emotional punches, this book will leave mystery lovers wanting more."

—Carter Wilson, *USA Today* bestselling author of
The Dead Girl in 2A and *Mister Tender's Girl*

PRAISE FOR *THE GRANDMOTHER PLOT*

"The characters are so richly detailed that they feel real."

—Kirkus Reviews

"The author does a remarkable job of combining tones, including sentimental and snarky, while being both wry and gently respectful... Cooney should win new fans with this one."

—Publishers Weekly

"More than a well-plotted mystery, which this is, this is a book that will make the reader think...to mull over issues long after they've finished the book. One strong recommendation: read the entire book through to the very end. The final encounters are as thought-provoking as the story itself."

—Mystery and Suspense Magazine

"Bestselling author Caroline B. Cooney has been perfecting the fine art of thriller writing for decades now, and her latest novel, *The Grandmother Plot*, will grip you from page one."

—PopSugar

PRAISE FOR *THE FACE ON THE MILK CARTON*

"Absorbing and convincing. Strong characterizations and suspenseful, impeccably paced action add to this novel's appeal."

—*Publishers Weekly*

"A real page-turner."

—*Kirkus Reviews*

"It's a gripper. You can't put it down until you've gone through the whole trauma with Janie Johnson, from that first moment of horrified recognition to the thoroughly satisfying conclusion."

—*Entertainment Weekly*

PRAISE FOR *THE RANSOM OF MERCY CARTER*

"Gripping and thought provoking."

—*Publishers Weekly*

PRAISE FOR *WHATEVER HAPPENED TO JANIE?*

"The power and nature of love is wrenchingly illustrated throughout this provocative novel... The emotions of its characters remain excruciatingly real."

—*Publishers Weekly*, Starred Review

"The gut-wrenching circumstances in which the characters find themselves are honestly conveyed."

—*Booklist*

PRAISE FOR *THE VOICE ON THE RADIO*

"Cooney's outstanding command of emotional tension has taken this novel to extraordinary heights."

—*School Library Journal*, Starred Review

PRAISE FOR *TWINS*

"[A] thriller master."

—*Publishers Weekly*

PRAISE FOR *NO SUCH PERSON*

"Full of twists and turns…has all the elements that keep young mystery lovers coming back for more."

—*School Library Journal*

"No one writes suspense like Cooney. Haunting, harrowing…hard to put down."

—*Kirkus Reviews*

"Cleverly plotted...rooted in suspense...fully satisfying. Mystery fans will be delighted."

—*Booklist*

"Jangling suspense juxtaposed with cozy details of family life keeps thriller master Cooney's latest zooming along."

—*Publishers Weekly*, Starred Review

"Cooney has hit it out of the ballpark yet again. A must read."

—*VOYA*

PRAISE FOR *DRIVER'S ED*

"As convincing as it is believable."

—*Publishers Weekly,* Starred Review

PRAISE FOR *DIAMONDS IN THE SHADOW*

"Crackling language and nail-biting cliffhangers provide an easy way into the novel's big ideas, transforming topics that can often seem distant and abstract into a grippingly immediate reading experience."

—*Publishers Weekly*, Starred Review

PRAISE FOR *HIT THE ROAD*

"Cooney masterfully combines nonstop, cleverly plotted action with heartfelt emotion."

—*Booklist,* Starred Review

"An unexpected, touching, and effective sojourn from the always entertaining Cooney."

—*Kirkus Reviews*

PRAISE FOR *REAR-VIEW MIRROR*

"So tightly written, so fast-moving that it's easy not to realize until the last paragraph is over that one hasn't been breathing all the while."

—*Washington Post*

PRAISE FOR *A FRIEND AT MIDNIGHT*

"Brimming with realistic characters, unexpected twists, and heart-warming redemptions, this is a superior read!"

—Melody Carlson, award-winning author

"Wrathful, courageous, resourceful, loving, and even occasionally lighthearted…"

—*Publishers Weekly,* Starred Review

Also by Caroline B. Cooney

THE WRONG
GOOD DEED

THE
WRONG
GOOD
DEED

A
NOVEL

CAROLINE B.
COONEY

Poisoned Pen
PRESS

Published by Poisoned Pen Press, an imprint of Sourcebooks
P.O. Box 4410, Naperville, Illinois 60567-4410
(630) 961-3900
sourcebooks.com

Library of Congress Cataloging-in-Publication Data

Names: Cooney, Caroline B, author.
Title: Wrong good deed : a novel / Caroline B. Cooney.
Description: Naperville, Illinois : Poisoned Pen Press, [2023]
Identifiers: LCCN 2021023668 (print) | LCCN 2021023669
(ebook) | (hardcover) | (trade paperback) | (epub)
Subjects: GSAFD: Mystery fiction.
Classification: LCC PS3553.O578 W76 2022 (print) | LCC PS3553.O578
 (ebook) | DDC 813/.54--dc23
LC record available at https://lccn.loc.gov/2021023668
LC ebook record available at https://lccn.loc.gov/2021023669

Printed and bound in the United States of America.
VP 10 9 8 7 6 5 4 3 2 1

SUNDAY

ONE

Clemmie and her friend Muffin sat in the sixth pew on the right side of the center aisle. They were getting to their feet for the last hymn when Muffin grabbed Clemmie's arm. "We have to get out of here!" she whispered. Her face was distorted with fear. "*Quickly!* Shove to your right."

Do we have a shooter? thought Clemmie. Her mouth went dry. *Should I scream a warning? Why isn't Muffin screaming?*

"That man on the far side of the center aisle?" said Muffin, her voice shaking. "Two pews down, two people in?"

The entire congregation was now standing. Clemmie was too short to see the aisle, let alone across it and down two pews, but she peered around anyway, looking for weapons. There had been a rash of church shootings this year. Many churches, including Trinity Hill, now had a policeman on duty in the parking lot Sunday

morning—squad car facing out, lights whirling. It was both comforting and appalling.

"I used to know him," said Muffin. "I don't want him to see me. We have to get out of here."

It wasn't a mass murderer? It was just somebody Muffin used to know? Clemmie sagged with leftover fear. Muffin elbowed her. It wasn't a gentle nudge. It was a sharp, urgent poke.

There were two couples between Clemmie and the far side aisle, and she wasn't about to shove them out of their pew just because Muffin had spotted an acquaintance. She shook her head and raised her hymnbook, hands trembling from the idea of a shooter.

Muffin leaned around her, tapped the closest husband on the shoulder, and said over the crescendo of the organ, "I'm so sorry. We have to leave early. Please excuse us."

They had come in Clemmie's car. If Muffin wanted to bail on church, Clemmie had to drive. She was forced to put her hymnbook back on the rack, gather her handbag and Bible, and slide past, murmuring apologies. Muffin strode out of the sanctuary, all but breaking into a run.

It was ridiculous. There were three or four hundred standing bodies between Muffin and the acquaintance. He couldn't possibly see what Muffin was doing, and if he'd been across the center aisle and two pews closer to the chancel, he wouldn't have had a view of Muffin to start with.

Few people noticed their exit. Although Clemmie herself sang

from the hymnbook, almost everybody else looked up at the huge screens. Didn't they have enough screens in their lives? They needed screens in church too? And the screens had only the words. Clemmie liked to read the notes, enjoy the chords, see who the composer was, and think about the year in which the hymn had been written.

Muffin hurried into the narthex. She cast a frantic look back at Clemmie, but to the police officer positioned at the exit door, she gave a pleasant smile.

So because of Danger Man, I have to skip the hymn and annoy our whole pew, thought Clemmie, but he isn't sufficiently dangerous to bring in the police.

The moment they were out of the building, Muffin said, "Run. He's going to follow me."

Muffin was, in fact, a runner. She was devoted to this awful practice, rising before dawn every day, dressing in leotards or tights or whatever they called them nowadays, running several miles on a strict pattern. She was as trim as a girl, although her face was deeply lined, so there was no hiding her age. Clemmie had never been interested in running. It was her belief that only flat-chested women could enjoy it anyway. Plus she didn't have the balance for it these days; she couldn't even wear high heels to church. What was the point in fashion if all your shoes were flats? She handed Muffin her purse because it held the key fob. Now Muffin could run ahead, duck inside the car, and maybe even hide, a frequent activity for Clemmie, who had spent half a century

living under somebody else's name, but not one she had ever pictured for Muffin.

Of the several church parking areas, Clemmie preferred the eastern end of the upper lot, close to the rear exit. It was a bit of a hike.

She and Muffin were wearing twin jackets, purchased at the L.L.Bean outlet store where they had stopped on a New England fall-color bus trip. The vivid indigo-blue jackets were tailored in an almost formal fashion. When the excitement of the purchase was over, Clemmie didn't actually want to wear hers; the gaudy color attracted too much attention. Clemmie detested attention. But Muffin often texted, asking Clemmie to wear it, and then they matched, like elderly cheerleaders.

Muffin peeled her jacket off, although the day was raw and chilly. "Take yours off, too, Helen. It's too bright. He'll see it."

Clemmie was still shaky from the thought of a shooter. How slow her response had been. What if it had been the real thing? She would have let the whole congregation down, checking and double-checking and not wanting to embarrass herself if she were wrong.

"Please," said Muffin. She was crying.

Astonished, Clemmie shrugged out of her jacket, folded it neatly, and carried it in front of her. Muffin darted ahead up stone stairs and scurried between rows of cars. Clemmie walked calmly, not looking back, because she wouldn't recognize Danger Man anyway.

She did not want to know the backstory to Muffin's flight. She had become the neighborhood visiting nurse, so to speak, and was

knee deep in sick people, friendless people, and people in pain. The sorrows of her past made Clemmie a soft touch. She never asked difficult or invasive questions since she would not answer such a question herself. She just listened and helped. Right now, however interesting Muffin's history might be, it could also present one more burden for Clemmie to shoulder and even solve.

By the time she reached her car, she was shivering from the unseasonable cold. She slid back into her jacket and eased behind the wheel, sinking onto the soft, fine leather. The seat with its wonderful memory adjusted itself in a leisurely way for a short driver with short legs. She retrieved her purse from Muffin because she liked to drive only when her handbag was within touching distance. She started the engine and pressed the button for the seat heater. So cozy to curl her spine into all that warmth.

Muffin actually lay down across the back seats. "Go, Helen!" she cried, her voice breaking. "Go, go, go!"

Clemmie headed toward the main road. She meant to go straight, but the light went red. There were several ways home to Sun City, so rather than wait and increase Muffin's distress, she took a right on red, mentally revising her route. Then she touched the navigation button and up came the wonderful map to reassure her. Cars these days were so much fun.

Half a mile later, she made another turn onto Shirley Road, not well traveled at any time, but on a late Sunday morning, entirely without traffic. The road was narrow and potholed, probably on

the county list for improvement, but road repair lists were long and not enough people lived here to put Shirley Road at the top. Most rural acreage in the county had been swallowed at a stunning rate by developments, condos, apartments, strip malls, gas stations, fast-food restaurants, and nail salons. But here on Shirley there were still a couple of marginal farms, with white-fenced pastures and flat, wet fields.

"Thank you, Helen," said Muffin in a weepy voice. "It was from a long time ago. I never expected to cross paths after all this time. It's one of the amazing things about a retirement village like Sun City. You're always bumping into some connection. People join the New York-New Jersey-Connecticut Club and find out that their kids' junior high principal lives here too. So it shouldn't surprise me that somebody from long ago would appear. Although you would think church would be safe."

Clemmie decided to take the next left onto Patterson Church Road. It was not the quickest way, but certainly the prettiest, because a few miles up were two charming little churches. One brick AME Zion, where her friend Gale went, and one clapboard Baptist.

Leggings! she thought. That's what leotards are called now.

Clemmie both loved and loathed the slow recall of old age. Not that your seventies were old these days. Seventies were the new fifties.

She caught up to a small gray pickup truck wandering slowly from one side of the road to the other. She assumed it was pothole

avoidance. There were two girls in the little cab, driving with the windows down, although it was not warm enough for that. Perhaps they were in love with how their long hair swirled out.

The turn from Shirley Road onto Patterson Church was angled slightly backward and required a serious slowdown. Patterson Church was narrow and had no verge, but was flanked by deep drainage ditches thick with weeds. Clemmie liked the 1930s air of this road—little old houses surrounded by haphazardly planted overgrown shrubbery, junked agricultural implements, and pansies planted in white-painted tires. Probably by next year it would sport several subdivisions, one of which would be gated, plus an apartment complex and the latest elementary school.

The little gray pickup failed to make the acute turn. Both driver-side wheels drove neatly into the invisible ditch. The truck tipped severely but evenly on its left. It happened slowly. If the girls were wearing seat belts, Clemmie doubted they would have a scratch. But there was no way out of that ditch except a tow.

Clemmie did not want to stop, what with Muffin crying quietly to herself in the back seat. But she was not the kind of person who failed to help people, especially since the ditch made this a Good Samaritan parallel if there ever was one. Clemmie braked gently. "Muffin, stay down."

"Helen! What are you doing?" Muffin whispered frantically. "Do not stop!"

The passenger door of the little truck opened with difficulty,

because of the extreme tilt, and out slid a very young girl, barely into her teens. She was thin and pretty with long, thin, pretty hair and clothing suitable for July. She was sobbing.

Clemmie came to a full stop and put down her window. "Is anyone hurt?"

"No. We're fine. But now what?" the girl wailed.

"Do you have your cell phone?"

The girl looked at her, like, *What—are you mental? Of course I have my cell phone.*

"Call your parents," said Clemmie, and the girl said, "No, no. No, I'm sure we'll be fine. Jayleen, we can get out of the ditch, can't we?" She turned huge eyes on Clemmie. "My sister's driving."

The sister now crawled out the passenger side, too, having no way to open the driver door. It was so awkward that both girls exploded in giggles. When Jayleen finally got herself upright on the pavement, she looked so young she couldn't have had her driver's license more than a minute.

"Helen!" whispered Muffin. "Keep going. They have their phones! They're not hurt!"

But Jayleen also got weepy and said, "Now what?"

"Call your parents," Clemmie repeated, and the sisters exchanged looks, like, *Then we'd be dead.*

Clemmie had been a Latin teacher for half a century, and still taught, which her friends at Sun City considered lunatic, and she liked teenagers. These two probably don't have permission to use

the truck, she thought. Or Jayleen really isn't old enough to drive. Or nobody has insurance. "I can't stay in the middle of the road," she told them. "I'll pull into that driveway and walk back and we'll decide what to do."

"No! You don't have to do that," said Jayleen. "We're fine, really. Aren't we, Jaymie?"

Clemmie drove a few hundred feet to the weedy gravel drive of a house set so far in that she could barely see it. To leave their driveway open, she had to park behind scary shrubbery that in warmer weather would be snake habitat.

"How could you?" asked Muffin, as if Clemmie had taken up human trafficking.

"Muffin, you're fine here. Nobody can see my car from the road, let alone spot you. And you don't have to get home quickly; you just had to leave church quickly. Read a book on your cell phone or something. I'll be back in a jiffy."

Two

The girls were now standing in the middle of the road, as if getting hit themselves would be preferable to calling anybody. They were clearly sisters, so pretty with their matching straw-like hair. "Did you reach your parents?" asked Clemmie.

"Let me try again," said Jaymie in a high fake voice. She played with her cell phone, but failed to tap the screen. "They're not answering," she said happily. She backed up against the gray tilted length of her petite truck and took a selfie. Jaymie did the same. They compared pictures and took selfies featuring them both.

"Do you have another phone number to try?" asked Clemmie.

Jayleen stepped up. "I'll call my father." She played with her phone. "No answer," she said sadly.

Whatever else the sisters' future included, it wasn't acting. Clemmie needed to get this show on the road, so she tapped her

own phone. "Nobody's hurt," she said to the voice that answered 911, "but there's been a one-vehicle accident at the corner of Shirley Road and Patterson Church. A small pickup truck is in the ditch, and the driver is a teenager who can't reach her parents. We don't need an ambulance, but we do need a trooper."

Jayleen and Jamie were horrified and furious. "We didn't say you could do that!" cried Jayleen. She actually stomped her foot.

If a teenage boy had been watching, he would fallen madly in love. Jayleen was adorable.

"Thank you, ma'am," said the telephone voice. "A trooper will be there soon. Is everybody safely out of the vehicle?"

"Yes."

Both girls were now frowning at their cell phones, as though surprised that the devices had not come to the rescue; that there was no app for a truck in a ditch. Well, actually, there probably was. "Do you have Triple A?" Clemmie asked.

Jayleen looked at her, like, *How would I know? That's stuff you old people do.*

A vehicle was approaching from the same turn off Shirley Road that Jayleen had missed. It was a big, shiny black SUV, high up off the road, all its windows shaded. It pulled up next to them and stopped.

Clemmie suddenly remembered Danger Man. Could he really exist? Had Clemmie even once glanced in her rearview mirror to see if anybody was following?

But the driver who rolled his window down was not even fifty.

He sported sunglasses, a bow tie, and a white button-down shirt. He could very well have come from the eleven o'clock service at Trinity Hill, which was traditional in spirit, liturgy, and clothing, as opposed to the earlier service where you wore and sang any old thing. But if he was chasing down indigo jackets, he would see that this particular indigo-jacket woman was a foot shorter than Muffin, much curvier, and wearing red lipstick and a black wig with tight curls, like an aged Betty Boop. Completely unlike long, lean, elegant Muffin. "You okay?" he called.

The girls glared.

"Thank you, yes," said Clemmie. "Nobody's hurt."

He looked around, obviously puzzled. "Where's *your* car?" he asked.

This was unsettling. Why did he care? Why would he not assume that Clemmie had also been in the truck? But the little gray truck was a two-person vehicle. Besides, she was wearing church clothes, while what little fabric the girls had chosen was ragged and silly in the way of today's adolescent fashions. They and Clemmie were not a match. She ignored his question because she had spent her life sidestepping questions and said, "A trooper is on the way."

"I'll just wait with you," he said. "You need flashers or there'll be another accident." He maneuvered his big car rather impressively, placed himself between the tilted truck and the intersection and put on his hazard lights. Only now did Clemmie see a silhouette at his side. He had a passenger. Could that be Danger Man? Not that

Clemmie believed in Danger Man, let alone his possible decision to bolt early from church, leap into his car, and race after a departing Avalon.

The man got out of his vehicle, walked back, and chatted with the girls. "You go to high school around here?"

Clemmie didn't like that; nothing about these girls was his business except their safety, so she interrupted and asked him, "What church do you go to?" In the South, this was a courteous and constant question, not the least intrusive.

He too sidestepped. "I'm from Charlotte," he said, as if referring to some distant place like Nova Scotia, instead of a city a dozen miles away. "Where do y'all live?"

"She lives in Sun City, I bet," said Jaymie, giving Clemmie a snarky look. "You can get there from here and she's old."

Clemmie had to laugh. "Good deduction," she said. "Not necessarily true. Old people can live anywhere."

Jaymie began complex line-dance steps, easing herself down the road and away from questions. Clemmie admired her poise, but wished the dance wasn't right down the center of the road. She looked at her watch. She wanted to be done with this fender bender and get Muffin home. Perhaps Good Samaritans were always left with such a problem: how long did you have to manage somebody else's disaster?

"You were the driver?" the man asked Jayleen.

She nodded.

"How did it happen?"

"Um. Well. The steering wheel. It sort of locked."

The man didn't hide his skepticism. "How could you tell?"

"None of your business," snapped Jayleen, and that exchange might have gone anywhere, except that the trooper pulled up. Lights twirling, but no siren, he parked without falling into the ditch, and now the pickup was protected at both ends by other people's vehicles. Jayleen and Jaymie looked at each other apprehensively. They both had such startling eyes.

"You're quick," Clemmie said to the officer.

He was not into small talk. "Is it your truck?" he asked.

"No. I was coming home after church and saw the accident happen. I called it in. Neither of the girls is hurt."

"And your car?"

She gestured. "I pulled into that driveway."

He nodded and said to the driver of the SUV, "Sir?"

"Another stranger driving by after church."

The trooper nodded a second time, dismissing them both. "I'll handle it now."

Clemmie didn't expect teenage girls to be grateful, but the officer could have said thank you. Slightly miffed, she turned to walk away and was surprised when the man from the SUV said courteously, "I'll just walk you to your car." He stepped alongside and she thought, Hmmm. It's broad daylight, there's a policeman here, and this man thinks I need an escort?

What if this really was the man from whom Muffin was fleeing? Perhaps Clemmie had made an incorrect assumption that Danger Man was also in his seventies. Perhaps he actually did want to see Clemmie's car. That had, after all, been his second question.

But he wouldn't care about her car. He'd care about her passenger.

The trooper was now questioning the girls. Their high nervous voices were like flutes, wavering and trembling.

Clemmie and the man from the SUV walked another few steps and Clemmie paused. She took a posture that said she was going no farther. "Thank you for stopping to help," she said, looking up at him. In her next life, Clemmie planned to be tall.

His sunglasses prevented her from looking into his eyes. If they crossed paths again, she would not recognize him.

"I just wanted you to know," he said softly, "that those girls are completely wasted. You did the right thing stopping, but you should just have called 911 and driven on. Teenagers as high as that— who knows how they might act? And you are a very small woman. Anything could have happened."

THREE

No wonder the girls hadn't wanted parents or cops. Clemmie had thought their silliness was panic about their parents' reaction, that the wide, fluttering eyes were some sisterly match. "Thank you," she said. "You're very kind." She waited. After a few beats, he wished her a pleasant day and walked back. When he had passed the officer and the girls and was almost at his own car, she crossed the road and hurried down the drive, mindful of every little stone on which she could turn an ankle. She should have recognized the drug factor, but Latin students were always the best kids. She rarely had problems with them, and they in turn rarely had problems like drugs. She was less aware than other high school teachers would be.

She was startled to find her car door locked. She'd almost forgotten Muffin, let alone that she was terrified and in hiding. Muffin clicked the locks open.

"Stay down, Muffin."

"I *am* staying down. I've been staying down for *hours*. What took you so long?"

"I'm so sorry. We had to wait for the trooper. Actually, he was very fast. He must have been in the area already."

Clemmie backed onto the grass and headed slowly out the driveway. She was still partly concealed by the heavy shrubbery when the black SUV drove slowly past. Whether the driver or passenger glanced her way, she could not tell because of its tinted windows. Just in case, she went the other direction, carefully edging past the police car and the girls, who glared at her. She retraced a mile to take a different way home.

"A man driving what I think was a Suburban also stopped to help," she told Muffin. "He came from the same direction as Trinity Hill and he was dressed for church. But he was young, Muffin. I don't think he could have been fifty. He did have a passenger, but I couldn't see that person."

"The person who frightened me would be a year or so younger than I am."

"In any event, the SUV went on up Patterson Church, but I've taken the other way and we're headed toward Harris Road. There's nobody behind us. You can sit up."

Muffin straightened, tugging at her clothes. She yanked on her long hair, ran her fingers through it, yanked again, and fastened it in a messy but fashionable knot. Clemmie had always yearned for long,

straight hair she could do cool things with. One of those dreams never to be realized, like becoming an adorable airline stewardess with whom pilots fell madly in love.

"You probably want an explanation," said Muffin.

But Clemmie had a difficult afternoon ahead. Her neighbor Bonnie, who had taken a spill in pickleball and snapped her ankle, was home in great pain, using a walker, and in such a bad mood that nobody liked visiting her. Clemmie had promised to provide lunch for Bonnie, which itself promised to be awful, because she was also bringing Gale. Gale's perfectly ordinary cataract surgery had resulted in such serious floaters that reading, driving, and everything else were now difficult. After lunch, Clemmie was taking another neighbor, Chip, to Memory Care to visit his beloved wife, whose Alzheimer's he had dealt with easily until he hurt his back and could no longer care for her at home. Since the bad back meant that he also couldn't drive, neighbors were hauling Chip back and forth for daily visits.

Life in your seventies and eighties was lived on the edge whether you wanted to be there or not.

"It's about my first husband," said Muffin.

Clemmie restrained herself from saying, "Ah, the old first husband story," and instead explained about having to fix lunch for Bonnie and Gale. "I need to drop you off and rush on, Muffin. I'm so glad everything worked out well today," she finished, although she didn't know what everything was, let alone whether it had worked out well.

Tomorrow was Monday, and there was school, but Clemmie had no classes to teach. Her high school had instituted block scheduling: odd, chunky rotating hours that might or might not be best for learning, but which did give her a three-day teaching week. Unfortunately, class days also rotated, so she was constantly checking the calendar to be sure she didn't confuse her on and off days. Having already completed her Tuesday teaching preparation, she could do whatever she chose on Monday.

She dropped Muffin in front of her little villa, drove two more blocks, hurried into her own small villa—Sun City's word for attached houses—and changed out of her church clothes. She didn't feel the usual peace from church, perhaps because she hadn't been there for the closing prayers. She fixed BLTs using that wonderful new product, precooked bacon, placed the sandwiches and the pineapple upside-down cake she had baked yesterday in a tote, threw in a bag of Fritos, drove one cul-de-sac over to get Gale, and drove to Bonnie's cul-de-sac.

Bonnie and Gale had met in water aerobics and discovered that they were both retired schoolteachers, widows, and nonstop talkers. Their favorite game was Rummikub, which Clemmie also played now and then, but they always slaughtered her.

Bonnie had the television on and the volume high.

If there was one thing that tired Clemmie out, it was the news. Just as so many women in Sun City had decided that five or six decades of cooking was enough and had informed their husbands that

21

from now on, they went to restaurants or bought takeout, Clemmie felt that six decades of news were enough. She had never had any effect upon the news—world, national, or local—and instead of becoming used to it, it hit her harder. In her younger years, she had subscribed to newspapers and weekly newsmagazines and kept up with everything. Now she knew that everything didn't care whether she kept up. She had retreated happily into the cocoon that was a retirement village. The news she cared about was who would be at cards and with whom she would carpool for ladies' lunch out.

Clemmie had neglected to school Bonnie in this outlook, and Bonnie was full of outrage, which in Bonnie took very little. Her outrage was widespread and covered pretty much the universe. "That ridiculous reporter! That lynching guy! I'm already sick of his nonsense," she sputtered, taking the plate of sandwiches Clemmie had brought. She frowned. "White bread, Helen? Really? You haven't moved on to whole wheat?"

Clemmie had had a chance to get rid of her other two names not long ago and she had dithered, because if outrage was Bonnie's middle name, dither was Clemmie's, and now it was too late. She would die here as Helen Stephens, and she would die in another state as Clementine Lakefield and in yet another as Clementine Murray. Oh well. Some other person would have to clean up that debris. Or not. Her various persona might float indefinitely, like plastic in the ocean.

"I couldn't agree more about that reporter," said Gale. "The idea that that lily-white, lily-livered, so-called reporter was lynched is

pathetic, not to mention insulting to real victims. It's a fiction to draw attention to himself and sell more books. Setting his lies in 1964 keeps him safe. How can anybody prove or disprove it now?"

"He isn't claiming he was *lynched*," said Bonnie, "because then he would be dead. It's stupider. He's claiming he was *almost* lynched."

With the television on so loud, they were shouting. Clemmie didn't get up to lower the volume, because she assumed that among all her other problems, Bonnie was deaf, refusing to admit it, and not about to get hearing aids. Bonnie and Gale were alike in so many ways, except skin color, that Clemmie thought Gale was probably deaf too.

"He says he escaped," said Bonnie.

"No, he doesn't. He says he was saved by a beautiful young girl with long, dark hair."

They all giggled. Of course she was young and beautiful. Who wanted to be saved by some overweight middle-aged woman in sweatpants?

"Eat faster," Clemmie said to Gale. "Very soon I'm driving Chip to Memory Care."

"That man is using you, Helen," said Bonnie. "He's using the whole pod. He keeps calling people to drive him up there and hang out while he feeds his wife a meal. How long does he expect to do this? The neighborhood is not responsible. Millie doesn't even know he's there."

"I love that Chip keeps visiting Millie," said Gale. "I'd drive him

every day if I could see well enough to drive. I have floaters, you know, because of that worthless ophthalmologist, and it's unforgivable but it turns out I can't even sue him because I signed a paper ahead of the surgery acknowledging that it has a degree of risk. And speaking of risk, did you hear about Susie Kennett? She is so worn out by her druggie daughter, I mean, it's been *years*, maybe even *decades*, and now the daughter's boyfriend and his whole criminal family are mooching off Susie. Anyway, she locked up her house and fled to some unknown location."

Clemmie had never met Susie Kennett, who lived in another pod (Sun City's slightly creepy word for neighborhood), but stories about the daughter's squalid existence circulated constantly. "Chip is expecting me in ten minutes, Gale. I'm wrapping up your sandwich for you."

"You can let me finish chewing, Helen. Chip isn't an emergency."

"The point is," said Bonnie, "that that reporter is lying, and furthermore, it's a pitiful second-rate lie, just to sell more books."

"What else is new?" asked Gale. "Everybody who writes a tell-all book tells lies to sell more of them." She began listing politicians whose books were full of lies. This was a fruitful topic and could last for hours, so Clemmie stood.

"The reporter got absolutely roasted on television last night," said Bonnie.

"I know, I watched," said Gale. "His story is full of holes. All that nonsense about four killers he couldn't identify fifty years ago

and can't identify now. Furthermore, they aren't killers because he's alive. And even more furthermore than that, he's white. When was a white man ever in danger of being lynched? There's people who want to lynch him now because he's trying to take over lynching."

Gale had graduated from a segregated high school somewhere local, and Clemmie would have liked an insider's view of desegregation in the Carolinas, but she didn't want it now. "I'm lea–ving," she said singsong.

"What's his name, anyway?" asked Bonnie. "I forget."

"Wait, Helen," said Gale. "What dessert did you bring?"

"Pineapple upside-down cake. If you want it, you have to stay here and then walk home."

"I better stay. Pineapple upside-down cake is bound to be fortifying."

"MacBurton Ward!" remembered Bonnie.

"You cheated. You Googled him," said Gale.

Clemmie hurried out of Bonnie's, drove around the corner, and pulled up at Chip's. The poor man was standing in his door, waiting. It was touching. There had never been a man in Clemmie's life who yearned so much for her company that he would drive to her side every day and hold her hand when she no longer recognized him. Clemmie blinked back tears, amazed that she could still be reduced to longing after all these years, and helped Chip into the front seat.

"That reporter was on yet another talk show," said Chip. "TV loves that guy. They get to sneer at him and undermine his story

but also prove their journalistic value by showing these appalling black-and-white photographs of real 1920s and '30s lynchings. This morning they had a historian who pointed out that the last verified lynching in South Carolina was in 1947. Therefore nobody tried to lynch MacBurton Ward in 1964, and furthermore, he's white as Elmer's Glue."

The word *verified* implied that there were *un*verified lynchings. Clemmie shuddered. "And have you gotten to know any of the other residents' families when you visit Millie?" she asked.

Chip laughed. "I gather you've topped out on discussions of MacBurton Ward."

"I never had a particle of interest. I'm not even reading a paper this year. I open my phone, scan headlines for ten minutes, and ask myself, 'Do I need to read about dissension in the U.S. Senate?' Probably not, since there's been dissension in the Senate for my entire life. Chip, there are whole continents I skip. It's very simplifying, like cleaning your closet."

"If I didn't have news and sports, I would have nothing. I miss Millie so much I can hardly stand it. And don't say anything about how she doesn't know me. Millie and I got married at eighteen and we're two of the lucky ones. We had rough times but they weren't very rough. We kissed and made up, whatever it was, and Millie was my rock and my joy. And you know what, Helen? She still is. You're my wonderful neighbor, taking me up there when I can't drive, and I'll sit with Millie and hold her hand and she won't even

glance my direction, because Alzheimer's has eaten everything. And I still love her."

"That's beautiful, Chip," Clemmie said, and it was. It was too late now for her to have anything like that. And too late to extricate herself from the name Helen Stephens. There had been valid reasons to keep it. There were still valid reasons. Just because she was tired of the reasons didn't mean they had evaporated. She wished she had a family on whose collective shoulder she could cry. Or a Chip.

"But that's also why I follow this MacBurton Ward story," said Chip. "It's something to think about besides the decay of my wife and my body."

FOUR

When Clemmie was finally home, all needy neighbors accounted for, she sank into her sofa's warm embrace. Could she summon the strength to fix herself dinner, or should she just have toast?

The doorbell rang.

She looked at her watch. Six o'clock on Sunday evening. Who could this be? She hauled herself up, opened her front door, and in trooped Virgie, Muffin, Marge, Phyllis, Fran, and Barbara Ann.

"You forgot, Helen," Fran accused her. "You're hosting Bible study this week."

The girls arranged themselves in her living room. Fran sat on the carpet, crossing her legs like the yoga instructor she was, demonstrating that she was a hundred times more flexible and healthier than anybody else except Muffin. Muffin usually tried to one-up Fran, but tonight she drooped in an armchair, exuding tragedy.

Gale had joined them once, but she went to Sunday School in her own church and also attended Bible study there on Wednesday evenings. From what Clemmie could tell, those groups were a lot more intense and scholarly than this one, so Gale didn't come again.

Clemmie slit open a cylinder of Ritz crackers, put these and some cheddar on a pretty little tray she'd made in pottery, although most things she made in pottery were ugly and cracked, and located napkins and paper dessert plates. Barbara Ann had brought a home-made coffee cake, which was bound to be delicious, because her baking leaned heavily toward butter, eggs, sugar, and cream. Barbara Ann arranged everything beautifully on the coffee table and sat on the straight chair because she had a bad back. Clemmie took the only remaining chair, unfortunately across from Muffin, who kept shooting her meaningful looks.

Of course, they had to be studying Acts, a short, exciting book not surprisingly full of action, featuring people with enough energy to trot from Jerusalem to the interior of Turkey or the coast of Greece and back while they were being arrested or else escaping arrest. Clemmie felt barely able to give everybody something to drink, especially the people who wanted a Coke, no, not real Coke, Diet Coke. No, not sweet tea, you know I never touch that. Unsweet.

Muffin's Bible was so well used its pages were falling out. She kept it in a dear little leather suitcase especially made for Bibles.

Retrieving a fluttering page, she said, "I can't buy a new Bible because I've written notes and references in all the margins and I'd lose them."

Clemmie would never deface any book with writing, never mind the Bible. She cut herself a generous slice of Barbara Ann's cake, which of course was utterly delicious. You might say *sinfully delicious* except that Barbara Ann had probably never committed a sin in her life. Clemmie didn't even try to follow the discussion Fran was leading but concentrated on not falling asleep. When exactly forty-five minutes had passed, she said, "That was so meaningful, Fran. Thank you. Barbara Ann, won't you say our closing prayer?"

Barbara Ann was a prayer warrior. You closed your eyes and sank into Barbara Ann's prayers, and Clemmie was in need. Barbara Ann thanked God for his many blessings and asked him to bless every needy neighbor, known and unknown: Bonnie, Gale, Chip, Millie, Susie.

She and Marge departed, arguing about who was the hostess next time. Phyllis and Fran tidied the kitchen and then finally left. Virgie was slow, shuffling her photocopied maps of Saint Paul's various journeys and frowning, as if looking for a lost grocery list.

Muffin started to zip up her little Bible suitcase, but lost her grip. The Bible fell out and splatted open at Virgie's feet.

"Why, Muffin," said Virgie, picking it up, "what a beautiful Bible!"

The binding, usually hidden inside the case, was an unusual forest-green leather with gold lettering on the bottom right front.

Clemmie, a compulsive reader, leaned forward to see what name had been imprinted, because it certainly wasn't *Muffin*.

CHRISTAPHINE ANGELIQUE REVERE.

Was it a secondhand Bible? A thrift-shop find?

"What an amazing name!" cried Virgie. "How do you pronounce it? Say it for me, Muffin."

"Please don't handle my Bible, Virgie. It's fragile." Muffin took it back and pulled the zipper emphatically.

Virgie rummaged around for a spiral notebook and pen. "Pronounce it for me, Muffin."

"I don't use my birth name. I've been Muffin since I was a baby."

"Say it," demanded Virgie, not noticing that she was seriously annoying Muffin. On the other hand, who would expect somebody to be protective of her birth name?

Well, me, for one, thought Clemmie.

After all these decades, a pang of loss brought tears to her eyes. She turned away to hide her emotion although the girls were not even faintly interested in her. It was the fate of one who hid; a sort of faceless existence came with the decision.

Muffin gritted her teeth. "Christa. Feen."

"Christaphine! How lovely. Muffin is your nickname then. Of course they wouldn't put a nickname on your Bible. Did you get the Bible when you were little and first joined the church? Did you join in third grade? That's when we joined." On a fresh notebook page, Virgie carefully printed CHRISTAPHINE ANGELIQUE REVERE.

Muffin seemed genuinely alarmed. "What are you doing?" she demanded.

"You know that I write articles for *Club News*." Virgie was extremely proud of her new publishing career. She wrote two paragraphs a month for the Sun City magazine about ladies' nine-hole golf. The magazine was quite professional, thick with advertising for golf carts and plantation shutters, and distributed free to each household. "You did so well in the last tournament. You got a hole in one, remember." Virgie frowned. "It was you, wasn't it?"

Muffin rolled her eyes. "Yes, it was me."

"It will be of such interest to the readers to know that your real name is so romantic. Christaphine Angelique Revere. I mean, it's an ocean away from Muffin."

"It's not my name. I got married. My name is Muffin Morgan."

Clemmie would have kept the name Christaphine and gotten rid of Muffin, but who was she, with three versions of herself, to question anybody's name choices? "Virgie," she said, herding them to the door, "we've just been studying Christianity. As in 'Do unto others,' etcetera. Muffin doesn't want you to use that name, so don't use it."

Virgie heaved a huge sigh, as if she had been ordered to clean toilets at the discount mall. She left with hugs and kisses, though, because Virgie, a true southerner, could neither greet nor depart without them.

Clemmie turned to find that, far from leaving, Muffin had taken over the sofa. She was holding the tissue box in her lap and crying.

"So here's my story," said Muffin.

FIVE

In the nineteen sixties, when Christaphine drove away from the town of Ferris, South Carolina, for the last time and became Muffin again, hiding one's past was relatively easy. More than half a century went by. Muffin had forgotten that she even had a past. Thrilled by retirement, she headed South for its pleasant climate and discovered the magic kingdom that was Sun City. She delighted in her new friends, the amazingly long list of activities awaiting her, and the warm, golden sunshine. Nineteen sixty-four was so long ago that she literally didn't notice she was moving to the vicinity of her own ancient history.

Sun City faced north and was really part of Charlotte, North Carolina. Muffin's past was more than a hundred miles, and light years of social change, south of her retirement community.

Muffin's past was Ferris.

The year was 1964.

When you thought of those hate-filled, pre-integration days, you couldn't believe you had been a bystander, let alone a participant. On Martin Luther King Day, you looked at those old newsreels and said to yourself, *No, no, we never behaved like that. Well, some people did. But not us. Never us.*

In Ferris all those years ago, MacBurton Ward had been that creature called an outside agitator, which now sounded like a washing machine. Tempers were hot, the air was hotter, hearts were racing, sweat pouring, rage visible. MacBurton Ward was just a college kid when he sauntered into town. Grinning, all casual and Yankee, laughing out loud at deep southern accents, unable to believe that grown men actually said *bidness* instead of *business*, he brandished his notebooks and camera like the weapons they were.

When Christaphine's father-in-law, Tommy Senior, referred to the colored residents of Ferris, his nouns and adjectives were literally unprintable. But MacBurton Ward wrote it all down, one ugly, derogatory word after another.

His first article was published in the *New York Herald Tribune*, which a few months earlier had published Martin Luther King's "Letter from Birmingham Jail" on the front page. Ward's article was picked up by news agencies around the country.

For the first time, Ferris men grasped what the North thought— that using perfectly ordinary synonyms for *Negro* was proof that white southerners were uncivilized barbarians who must be brought

to heel by federal decree. Ward took photographs of For Sale signs in front of houses specifying Whites Only; of restaurant signs excluding coloreds. He found old photographs of the recently bulldozed black elementary school that hadn't had running water, the kids squatting over a trench behind the playing fields, which themselves were just meadows mowed now and then. He didn't take a photograph of the colored library entrance because there wasn't one.

Ferris was isolated. Back then, any Yankee was noticeable, whereas these days, no town was isolated. There'd been so much migration from the North and Midwest in the last several decades; so many retirees, immigrants, and new hires. The advent of air-conditioning had changed everything anyway. Prosperity brought exploding employment, vast subdivisions, and endless shopping strips. Little old towns were swallowed, their original main streets hard to find. The nineteen fifties and sixties left few traces. Old buildings and neighborhoods were gone and old attitudes disappeared or were carefully hidden.

But after all this time, MacBurton Ward had suddenly reappeared, with a far larger stage than anything that existed in 1964. Facebook, Twitter, television and radio talk shows. He was the sort of non-news that fascinated America. He would last a week or two and then be eclipsed by some celebrity scandal. Ward had a mission. He wanted to know who they were—those four men he claimed had planned his murder.

It was unlikely that MacBurton Ward could turn up even one

name, let alone four. It was impossible for him to find a shred of proof since nothing had happened. He needed the one and only witness to his unlikely tale—that beautiful girl with the long, dark hair.

When Muffin thought of the early sixties in South Carolina, she thought of heat. There wasn't yet air-conditioning in cars, or the town hall, in schools or at home. Her husband, Tommy, had installed a window unit in their bedroom, and sometimes she just camped there so she could breathe. Or you could go to the movies or Belk's, the department store chain she still loved. Other than that, you sweated.

You never encountered sweat any more. You never had great clots of wet clothing sticking to your back and thighs and underarms. You never wiped your face with a cotton hanky, essential because mopping up perspiration with paper tissue just turned the tissue to glop. You no longer carried a cardboard fan to church or aimed your little black metal desk fan at your face.

Her mother-in-law had been teaching her to knit, and they were both making were baby blankets. Eleanor Nearing had chosen fine yellow and white yarn. Christaphine's fingers stuck to it in the humidity and the heat. An hour's work hardly increased the blanket by half an inch. Mother Eleanor insisted that Christaphine was getting better at womanly skills.

But not the one that counted.

Christaphine had failed to get pregnant, and everyone was getting anxious, especially Tommy, who was a very lusty man. He loved

her; he was dealing with her failure, trying to remain courteous, because he was a gentleman and this was his dear wife. But no baby? How could that be, after all those wild nights and crazy long lunches? He wanted a whole stable of children. Boys, of course, but a girl or two as well.

Sunday afternoons, it was Tommy's habit to go for long country drives. He had bought a 1963 Corvette new last year. Red, of course. He didn't drive it for work; he drove his pickup for work. The Corvette was for show. Sunday afternoons, when Tommy cruised, he didn't take the Corvette on gravel or dirt roads, which was most of them back then. He worried about the finish, and anyway, you couldn't go fast on such a road.

So Christaphine had been surprised that Sunday when he suddenly turned down a narrow, weed-wrapped, unpaved road she'd never noticed before, way out in the country. They lurched over ruts, and the Corvette was not a car designed for such a surface. Tommy hunched over the wheel, wearing a hot, excited look, and she thought, He's planned something romantic.

Or, more likely, he planned to race somebody out here; they'd found a long, straight, level stretch and his buddies would be there in their cars, not that anybody had a car to match Tommy's Corvette.

She stared out the window and felt nervous, even with Tommy beside her. It was empty, unused country. It wasn't farmed. It wasn't inhabited. It was just there. The shoots of young trees grew too close and too low, defeated by drought. After a good rain, this road would

be one long, scary mudhole. Tommy turned onto a dirt track she thought was probably an abandoned farm lane. The soil here had always been poor, and the fields had been ruined by bad farming practices. The lane had not been graded in years. Maybe decades. Weeds had taken over the middle of the track and were closing in on the edges. It was the wrong territory for the Corvette. The fields vanished, the woods closed in, and the road, if you could call it that, had a dark, dangerous feel, as if somebody with a shotgun lay in wait. The car crawled forward, avoiding branches and pits and tilts.

They dead-ended at another road-like surface. There were no more woods, just old dead fields baking in the sun. Tommy paused. The wind blew dust ghosts up and down the empty lane. Facing them was the ruined foundation of some old house, although *foundation* was too grand a word for the stacks of fieldstones that had once supported joists. She imagined the chickens, stray dogs, and rats that had once occupied the space beneath that long-gone shack.

She gagged, swallowed hard, and talked herself out of nausea.

The vanished little house had had shade, because in its side yard stood an enormous oak. Thick, strong branches supported a great, green dusty umbrella of leaves. It was the only successful vegetation near the road. Way behind it, across the fields, another dark, awful woods leaned forward.

Tommy nodded to himself. Suddenly he was smiling at her. "So, my darling Christaphine." He loved her name. He never abbreviated it. He didn't use the nickname Muffin because he'd never heard it.

She dropped it at college, where he met her—the college she'd quit after one semester, eager to rush into marriage with Tommy. "Left or right, babe?" he asked.

Her hands were cold, although the Corvette was stationary and she was dripping with perspiration. "Which direction gets us to civilization faster?"

He laughed. Tommy had a wonderful laugh. It was a major reason for falling in love with him; when Tommy laughed, everyone laughed. It was a collecting laugh. People wanted to stand close and share it. "We're pretty far from anything, Christaphine. But left eventually goes back to the highway. Lotta turns. Right eventually leads to Pinch Creek."

Pinch Creek was not a town, but a remote country store, which was an occasional Sunday afternoon drive destination. Kids rode their horses to the store and got Cokes. Adults picked up fried chicken. She felt a little better, knowing that Pinch Creek was out there. But the right turn also looked scarier, as if it might peter out long before they reached Pinch Creek, or the car would snap in half in some awful ditch, or a fallen pine would block the road, and they'd have to back up for miles. Christaphine couldn't back a car. She had to park facing outward at the market or she could never leave.

Tommy turned left. She closed her eyes in relief, and even then she knew that she was choosing not to know, because that was what wives here did: they didn't know. But husbands always left clues; it was part of the game.

Clemmie wanted to get to her feet, chuckle in a friendly way, tell Muffin to head on home and they could talk another time. She felt as if Muffin was going to assault her with some awful sweaty truth. But even as Muffin's story accelerated toward nightmare, Clemmie knew that she ought to listen, that it mattered.

In any event, Muffin wasn't aware of Clemmie now. She was inside her past.

SIX

When Tommy finally drove home, Christaphine prepared for her Monday evening library board meeting. She was from the mountains of Virginia, and very much an outsider, although as Tommy Nearing's wife and Tommy Senior's daughter-in-law, she had been warmly welcomed. She'd been thrilled to be asked to serve on the library board because she was so young and inexperienced, and although she was a great reader, basically she knew nothing. She was unsettled to find that board members were quitting as fast as they could because the time had come to integrate the library.

The Colored Library consisted of two small rooms that backed onto the beautiful, spacious rooms of the regular library. The entrance to those two rooms was through the head librarian's office, so the real patrons, the white ones, never even knew about it. Only staff ever went in there.

The Colored Library had its own book collection, which Muffin had never seen because the board had discarded every book prior to her arrival in town. She had seen only the empty rooms. Colored people, of course, could not enter the library; they went to a window on their side of the building, invisible to white patrons who parked out front, and they knocked. The colored drinking fountain was out there, too, as a kindness. If a librarian were free and felt like it, she would find a book for them and pass it through the window. The coloreds had no way of knowing what was in their collection because they had no card catalog, so Muffin couldn't quite picture how it worked.

The Ferris librarian, realizing that none of the coloreds' books were in good enough condition to add to the permanent collection, had completed the first step in merging libraries: wholesale discard. Or perhaps, Muffin thought, but didn't ask for verification, the library board didn't want books with Negro fingerprints mixed in with the white books. Her own village in Virginia had never had the slightest problem with integration. Of course, it had been entirely white, which made it easier.

It had been a year since the discards; a year during which no colored person could borrow a book. The librarian, a woman of courage, wanted to set a date for opening the doors of the real library to coloreds. Many Carolina towns had already opened their libraries, often without announcements or signage, just easing silently into integration.

In Ferris, that date would be far off.

Her father-in-law had instructed her to vote against setting any date at all. No library in his town was going to admit a colored. They weren't smart enough anyway. When she said she planned to vote in favor of opening, Tommy's daddy said gently that the only the reason sweet little Christaphine had been put on the board was to vote against it. The board understood that she would obey her father-in-law; that's why they wanted her.

She had not even turned twenty-one. She didn't want to think about hard things. She wanted to learn how to bake and knit and keep a lovely home for Tommy and, above all, have babies. But what she had was a library board meeting. Where she would have to vote for the wrong thing. Because surely it was wrong to keep half the town from reading.

When she asked her husband to back her up, Tommy was as amazed as if she had suggested diving to the *Titanic*. "My daddy told you what to do," he said courteously, because he was always courteous, just like his father. Then he walked away from her, because that was how Nearing men ended conversations with their women; they finished and they left.

The *libraries* had been separate? Their *book collections* had been separate?

Clemmie had known about separate schools and segregated

restaurants, but she had never pictured libraries refusing readers. She had even forgotten the noun *colored* because its usage had been eclipsed over the years by African American and now Black. She thought of Gale. Given her age, she must have been insulted and hurt by people like Tommy's family. Clemmie didn't want to think about it. She preferred civilized thoughts about civilized people, and now Muffin was going to tell a story about savagery.

Whose? Her husband's? Her in-laws'?

Or Muffin's own?

But the library board meeting was canceled. Christaphine didn't have to choose after all. It wasn't canceled because the vote not to integrate was in danger; nobody still on that board would vote in favor of integrating.

It was canceled because MacBurton Ward announced that he was coming to the meeting. No surprise, since he had attended the last week's school board meeting, at which the school board announced the merger of one black and one white elementary school. This was solely to pacify the feds. That particular colored school was the one bulldozed prior to the arrival of the outside agitator, and the town had built an addition (using federal funds, which was a hoot) to the grade school where the white trash lived. It was a pretty good plan, Tommy Senior said, because white trash could be counted on to fight back. Baseball bats, rocks, whatever it took. The merger did not

involve busing because kids walked to school. To be sure, the colored kids would have a long walk, but that was just more footage for the white parents to line up.

Nobody said what the white parents would line up for.

The biggest problem down the road gripped Tommy Senior and his brother, Ev, and they discussed it constantly. What would happen when the feds demanded to have the colored high school closed down? When they were forced to merge high schools? What about, say, football? White high school football players sharing a locker room, showers, practices, and games with colored? It didn't bear thinking of.

Supposedly Ev had stomped away from one of the brothers' shouting sessions, gone to his used car dealership, and taken out his rage on a black employee. Supposedly Ev snapped the man's forearm. The man's "crime" could have been anything or nothing. He might just have uttered the word *football*.

"I didn't ask for details," said Muffin to Clemmie. "I didn't want to know. I never wanted to see Ev in action. I was afraid of him. Everybody was afraid of him."

Clemmie had once been afraid of a man. The memory of her helplessness left her trembling for the black man so helpless that he had to allow his white boss to break his arm.

National pressure to integrate was intense, said Muffin, which simply built the fury in Ferris. How dare you interfere? These are our tax dollars, our schools, our decisions. And we're not white supremacists. It's just that coloreds—they're not up to it. They're good enough for fields and factories. Not for sitting next to our children, pretending they can learn like real people.

Northern newspapers described southern towns as "facing high racial tension."

"If they'd stay out of our bidness," Tommy Senior said, "there wouldn't be any tension."

And now this scrawny, arrogant city boy MacBurton Ward planned to attend every meeting of every town board. Where, said Tommy Senior, he would quote. Publicize.

Twist.

The boys were meeting at Christaphine and Tommy's house that Monday night, and Tommy had expected his bride to be away at her library board meeting. Her presence was not welcome. Tommy told her to set out the desserts that Stefanie, their help, had baked, and then go visit a girlfriend. She asked if she could stay in the bedroom, knitting. Tommy frowned, but finally said, "If you watch TV." They had two televisions, an extraordinary indulgence, but Tommy didn't like to miss anything.

She knew that watching TV was for noise. She was not to overhear anything. And she didn't *want* to hear anything. That was also the role of wives: not hearing.

After years of fading away, in 1964 the KKK was experiencing an impressive resurgence. There were billboards on the highway advertising membership, even giving the phone number to call if you wanted to join. Tommy Senior said everything was infiltrated these days, and probably the only people to call that number now were FBI. So the boys didn't join the KKK like their fathers, but got into ROWP, Rights of White People, one of several alternates. ROWP and the KKK and Ferris and everybody else faced a deadline: President Lyndon B. Johnson had proposed a nationwide "civil rights" bill and the vote was coming up.

"Rights?" Tommy Senior kept saying. "Give them rights and we'll lose ours."

———————

Clemmie had never lived in the South Carolina Muffin was describing. Her experience was with the great, good heart of the South: kinder, warmer, and more courteous than anywhere else she had lived. Certainly more willing to work to defeat racism than the northern states she had known. She had wept over the slaughter of that Bible study class at Mother Emanuel AME Church in Charleston and stood in awe of the parish as it continued to extend love.

Muffin was softening the real adjectives and nouns of that grim time and place where she had landed as a bride, omitting what Tommy and Ev would really have said about their black neighbors,

and Clemmie was grateful. But even in the omission her home felt stained, as if she would have to repaint after Muffin left.

Christaphine had set out dessert plates and forks and napkins and lined them up beside the pecan pie and the pineapple casserole. She perked coffee, although nobody was going to have coffee, because Tommy had picked up enough six-packs for an army. When he got there, Tommy's cousin, Haven, who was even younger than she was, told her how pretty she looked, and Tommy's buddy Daniel said she looked like a million bucks, and Tommy's friend Webb said, "Pecan pie!"

She went into the bedroom and turned on the TV good and loud.

There was no such thing as a master bedroom back then. There were just biggish bedrooms and littler ones. The only bathroom, small with mint-green tiles, was across the hall. Eventually, she had to go to the bathroom. She stood at her door, listening, and then slowly and carefully opened it, tiptoed quickly across the hall and closed the bathroom door gently behind her. She tried to go fast in case one of the boys needed the toilet. When she was done, she crept back to her room.

The boys were laughing the deep chortles of drunks who were pleased with themselves.

The following morning was Tuesday.

She had chosen Tuesday for her appointment because on Tuesdays, Tommy generally worked a ten-hour day at his daddy's John Deere dealership. Christaphine would have loved to work there, too, but when she asked for a job, Tommy Senior just patted her bottom. He was a little bit handsy.

After a breakfast of runny eggs with hot sauce, country ham, very dark toast, and grits sprinkled heavily with pepper—the only meal she cooked, because the help did the real cooking—Tommy said, "Fix me a bag lunch." She wrapped two sandwiches and the last slab of pie in wax paper and lowered them carefully into a small brown paper bag.

"Noon," said Tommy softly. "We figure on noon." They kissed goodbye, and since it was Tommy, the kiss lasted and almost required a bedroom, but he said he really had to run, which he surely regretted, but "Tonight, my darling Christaphine, I'll be in a great mood. We'll celebrate."

Two minutes after his pickup was out the driveway, she was out the driveway in her Ford Country Squire.

SEVEN

If she went to the Nearing family doctor here in Ferris, her mother-in-law would know immediately; in fact, would *already* know, even before Christaphine went, because Mother Eleanor was friends with the nurse. The concept of patient privacy wasn't to arrive for many years, so the nurse would have phoned her up and said, "Eleanor, honey, little Chrissy's coming in for a pregnancy test. You comin' too?"

No. She had to get the test elsewhere, and be alone for the heartbreak if she was wrong, and not have to discuss her failure yet again with her disappointed in-laws and husband. So she made an appointment with an out-of-town obstetrician. Rejecting Mother Eleanor's doctor felt like sin. She couldn't imagine explaining herself.

The Ford Country Squire was as long as a truck and as heavy as a building, with big white eyebrows shading the headlights. Tommy

had bought it for her right after their honeymoon, because it would have room for all their future kids. All that was required was for Christaphine to produce them.

She focused on the drive. It wasn't that far, really, but towns in the rural Carolinas were very separated. There was no sprawl, no overlap. You had a village, then you had country. A dozen miles on, you were in another world. Everybody was town-proud. *My town is better than your town.* It was why some towns gritted their teeth and pulled off integration with a modicum of trouble: they couldn't bear to have ugly things said about or happening in their town. It was why other towns, like Ferris, were never giving in: they weren't having their town standards lowered.

She thought about the talk she'd overheard when she crossed the bedroom hall last night. She could do nothing about it. She had to stop worrying. But worry was almost blinding her.

The boys won't really do anything to MacBurton Ward, she told herself. They'll scare him. Make him soil his pants. Make him cry and beg. And he will. City boys are weak. They'll kick him out of the truck by the side of a road, drive away laughing, and that'll be that. Because he's white. "You kill a colored," Tommy Senior had once said, "same as killing deer." Which meant, Christaphine figured, that killing a white man was still murder.

So she didn't have to worry. Nothing would really happen to MacBurton Ward.

Once she had argued with Tommy about ROWP. He got so

angry so fast. He grabbed her shoulders as if to shake her. Then he pulled back, walked away, and didn't come home that night. What would he do to her if she called somebody to warn them about the plans for MacBurton Ward? Except…who would she call? The police in town were Tommy Senior's best friends.

Only days ago, three civil rights workers had disappeared in Mississippi. ("Come on," snorted Tommy Senior. "They weren't *working*.") Last night, Tommy had laughed so hard about those missing "workers." He hadn't used his wonderful collection laugh; last night his laugh had been sly and vicious. She wasn't exactly afraid of the four boys gathered in her living room, but she was.

My daddy says people like MacBurton Ward should be shot, Haven said last night. His daddy was Tommy's Uncle Ev, a man so rough that Muffin almost hid behind her husband or her mother-in-law when Ev was around.

My daddy says shooting's too good for 'em, said her Tommy. *Happens too quick*.

When she finally arrived at the doctor's office, she concentrated on parking the massive car. Then she concentrated on filling out her medical information sheet. Then she concentrated on getting through the exam. When he tells me I'm not going to have a baby, I won't cry. I'll say *Thank you, sir*, because I am a lady.

The doctor said, "Mrs. Nearing, you're so excited, your pulse is racing."

I'm not excited. I'm scared. Would Tommy and the boys really and truly…?

She erased the isolated tree, the scary dusty lane, the tilting rock piles carrying the ghost of a house, and looked up at the doctor, a little girl trusting the man to tell her what to do next.

"You're going to have a baby," he said, beaming. He gave her the due date and a sheet of instructions. His secretary made her next appointment. Everybody was laughing and happy for her, and she was happy, too, and when she got outside and was close to the station wagon, all she could see was dust and mud caking the wood panels, and she thought of the dust of that empty road, and the dark of that distant woods, and she thought, *Noon.*

It's possible that at noon, my husband will terrify a reporter and run him out of town.

It's possible that at noon, my husband will lynch him.

You didn't lynch white people. If the boys decided killing was what they needed to do, they'd shoot him, not hang him. But Tommy Senior had said that shooting was too good for MacBurton Ward, and Young Tommy obeyed his daddy.

She wondered how those Mississippi people had gotten rid of their three bodies. She wondered how the boys would get rid of MacBurton Ward's. But she probably knew. Way back beyond that oak was a deep woods where no doubt the boys had hunted.

She drove faster.

She tried to think of the joy of having a baby. Mother Eleanor wanted a girl because there was so much shopping and matching of colors and knitting of sweet little hats. But Tommy would be disappointed in a girl.

53

Her heart raced like the V-8 engine. By now they'd have picked up Ward. By now they'd be driving down that lane. They'd be in their trucks. What would they wear? Street clothes? Sheets?

Why had Tommy taken her and the Corvette out there Sunday afternoon? So she would know? So she would be part of it? So they would be linked forever in silence?

She thought about God. Her pastor used to say to the youth group, If you have to keep silent about it, don't do it.

Lord, Lord.

There would be a lot of guns. Every pickup had a gun rack. Tommy Senior and his brother, Ev, had taken Tommy and Haven hunting as soon as they were big enough to lift a shotgun. Hunting seasons marked out their year as surely as Thanksgiving and Christmas marked out hers.

She thought of the doctor's instructions. Stay peaceful and calm. No extra exertion. Be careful on stairs. Walk daily at a reasonable pace. Don't get too much sun. Drink milk.

She thought, *My baby's father will be a murderer.*

She actually screamed, and her own scream frightened her even more than she was already frightened. She rolled the window all the way down to let the wind whip over her face and through her hair and maybe cleanse her thoughts.

I knew all along. Tommy wanted me to know. And also not to know.

She was sobbing now, driving too fast to fish around in her pocketbook for a hanky. She used her sleeve.

My baby's father will be a murderer.

She found the scary rural lane and ripped down it. The Country Squire hardly noticed the ruts that had threatened the Corvette. She had the windows open so she could breathe, but dust clouds swept through and choked her.

Maybe she was making it all up. Maybe Tommy was at work. Maybe the T intersection would be empty.

And indeed, when the great oak tree came into view, her heart leaped with relief. No trucks were parked there. Tommy wasn't going to do anything to anybody!

I was wrong. Oh, thank you, God, I was wrong.

She would never tell anybody what she had suspected. She would erase every thought. She would knit like a madwoman because she felt like one right now.

But then she saw a line of tall, white shapes, the whiteness puffing and then sagging in the wind, and she knew that the boys had parked where their trucks couldn't be seen, where a reporter getting a brief glimpse couldn't memorize plates and makes and year.

If they had been KKK, they'd have had that terrifying head covering: the cruel sharp cone, the eyeholes of hell staring out, the capelike hem falling to the shoulders and down the chest, and under that, a sort of choir robe, because they were singing the songs of murder.

But these four were literally wrapped from head to toe in white sheets. White bandannas covered their faces, and bandannas tied around their foreheads kept the sheets in place.

They had planned their costumes.

They had practiced.

A fifth man, still safely on the ground, held his brimmed hat in one hand. In his other hand was a fat rope that hung from one of the great branches of the oak. They were making him help in his own hanging.

She was sobbing now as well as screaming, her foot pressing harder on the accelerator, not less.

She was so afraid.

Afraid of what her marriage would be after this.

Afraid that this action, the opposite of doctor's orders, would make her lose the baby.

Afraid that the boys, in their rage at being interrupted, would shoot after all.

At her.

She leaned on the horn, again screaming out her window, or perhaps she had never stopped screaming. For a moment, they just stood there as the huge, heavy wagon raced straight toward them and the horn blared. She didn't slow. At last the four in their sheets leaped out of her way, one of them tangling in his sheet and falling, and then she braked hard, skidding in a tight turn, screaming, "Get in the car!"

The Country Squire slewed wildly. MacBurton Ward dropped the rope, ripped open her back door—thank God he chose the back door, what would she have done if he'd gotten in front with her—and

she was racing away, taking the rutted, scary, unknown road to Pinch Creek only because the car ended up facing that way. "Close the door!" she screamed at him. "Get down!"

The heavy door flapped madly but he got hold of it at last.

The road was far worse than she could have imagined. It was only road-ish, with deep ruts and red clay dust and dried-up piles of manure. Weeds crept around and waved in the wind or lay dead and rusty looking. Potholes jounced the entire car. She flew on, the wagon banging and whapping and she thought, What if the axle snaps?

The car flung her into the air. It had none of those newfangled seat belts. Tommy said they were for sissies. She curled her tongue inside her mouth and gritted her teeth to keep from biting her tongue, but her mouth opened anyway because she couldn't stop screaming.

Out of nowhere, with no warning, the trail ended.

The car spurted onto a regular road, which she hadn't even seen coming, and she braked ferociously, leaving a serious patch and barely missing trees. She ended facing left, heading north, away from Ferris. The car felt intact. There was no traffic, which was good, because she had filled the entire pavement making the turn. But in those days, there really wasn't anything in the countryside you could call traffic. There were just other cars now and then.

One thing you could say for a V-8: it could go. She floored it, reaching a speed too scary even for her present mood. She lifted her foot a little.

Up ahead, a sign indicated an intersection. She had no idea what the crossroad might be.

She could smell the reporter. Urine and shit. The boys had gotten their wish. They had scared him. In her rearview mirror, she saw him starting to sit up.

She suddenly realized she had a bigger problem than the boys. The reporter would want to report this. "Stay down! They're right behind us!" she screamed.

She could not be in his newspaper. It would bring shame on her whole family. She would be shunned and hated.

I'll be shunned and hated anyway, she thought.

And then it hit her, knowledge so awful, so deep, so painful that she began crying instead of screaming.

I can't go home.

She who had so joyfully promised to love, honor, cherish, and obey Tommy Nearing, she who was going to have their baby, had to drive out of his life.

No, no, I'll think of something. There has to be something. It's my home. He's my husband.

"Thank you," said the man fervently from the back seat. "Who are you?" he croaked. "What's your name? Why did you save me?"

He was interviewing her, right here in her own car. "They have guns," she cried. "Stay down. I can't talk. I have to drive."

On the seat beside her was a hat. She had hats for church or for warding off the sun, because burns, tans, and freckles were not

attractive. Her emergency car hat, for when the sun was in her eyes, or they stopped unexpectedly and she needed to look nice, was ivory with an asymmetrical wide brim. It had ivory ribbons and an uncomfortable elastic that snapped under the chin. She drove without hands for a moment, settling the hat on her hair, tilting it to hide her face. The reporter could have glimpsed her when she drove up to the tree, but it wouldn't have been much of a glimpse; they'd all have been way too worried about being hit by the vehicle to think about the driver. Right now, crouched down low in the back seat, he couldn't see her at all. The hat would protect her when she had to get him out of the car.

She was crying steadily now, ordinary soundless girl tears.

She didn't know where Pinch Creek country store might be, but not here. She was probably way north of it. Tommy did all the driving except when she went for groceries or visiting. She didn't know the roads. At this outrageous speed, though, she had covered a lot of miles. The intersection was far behind, and she was approaching the outskirts of some town.

If the boys had parked away from the tree because they didn't want the reporter to see their license plates, then they were planning to release him. Because if they were planning to kill him, what difference would seeing anything make?

No, that didn't work. They would never release him because then he'd tell his story. They would want their fathers and friends to know what they'd done, but they wouldn't want the *Herald Tribune*

to know. They must have parked out of sight because it added to the fun.

She recognized a building. Amazingly, she knew where she was. She had just been to the obstetrician here. She couldn't quite think where she was in relation to Main Street but she did know there was a Howard Johnson's in this town. She kept her eyes peeled for the orange roof. She remembered now that this Howard Johnson's was still segregated.

When he gets to a phone, he'll call the police, she thought. Or maybe not. He'd never trust a southern cop. Besides, he won't want anybody to see that he soiled himself. Somehow he'll try to get dry and presentable. I have to get him out of my car without him looking at me or my license plate because it's bad enough already. I can't add police looking for me, if he's fool enough to think they'd help him instead of laughing themselves sick.

She organized her lies and spoke to him again. "They couldn't go as fast as we did over that bad road, but they're catching up."

She actually heard him gulp.

"I can see them in the mirror, way back," she lied. "I'll slow down enough so you don't get killed when you jump out. You jump when I say so, slam the door behind you, and run to your right. One block over is a Howard Johnson's. You'll be safe there. I'll keep on driving so they won't realize that you're not in the car anymore."

She added more lies. Unless they weren't lies. "They didn't get you back there, but they won't miss a second time. They'll shoot you

whether there's anybody around to witness it or not. No one will testify against them. Anybody sees, they'll clap. You have to *run*."

"Okay." His voice broke. He sounded like a girl.

"Get ready."

"I'm ready."

She braked. "Go! Go now!"

He wrenched open the car door, stumbled out, slammed it, and ran crouched, as if ducking bullets. She floored the accelerator, which in a car this powerful was fun even in these circumstances.

There was nobody else on the road.

Nobody behind her. Nobody in front of her.

She drove on, picked up a road important enough to have double painted lines, and headed east. She found another main road, and another one. An hour later, she had reached I-95. The entire eastern seaboard was off that interstate.

Now what?

She had done a good deed. But since Tommy thought that lynching a reporter was a good deed, he would never see that she was saving him from being a murderer.

What explanation could Tommy give if his wife never came home?

But I have to go home! It's my home.

She took the northbound entrance.

The next exit would surely have a gas station. The gas station would surely have a pay phone. She would call Tommy. *Hi, honey. Don't be mad.*

Don't be mad? When she had kidnapped his kidnap victim? Left him holding the noose, as it were? Shamed him in front of his best friends? Left him beaten by a one-hundred-ten-pound girl? What could he possibly say to his scary father and even scarier uncle? Men who had ordered him to kill? *Oh yeah, my wife drove off with him. I was helpless.*

EIGHT

Muffin's stories crawled on Clemmie's skin like red ants, biting viciously. Clemmie had taught high school in Akron, Ohio, back when they too had had violent race conflict. She remembered the boiling of hearts and the cooling of kindness, her own confusion of the soul because she had been that questionable thing: the bystander.

When Clemmie thought of the violence of the integration years, she always thought first of Birmingham: four little girls in their four little Sunday dresses, murdered by the bomb planted in their church. The KKK had been proudly responsible.

Imagine marrying into a family only to discover that the KKK was their hobby. Imagine listening to this credo night after night, every dinner an hour in which to spew hatred. What courage Muffin had shown! One young, obedient wife against four angry men who undoubtedly had gun racks in their trucks.

Muffin had risked all for a stranger. It was magnificent. "Bravo," said Clemmie. "That was truly a noble deed, Muffin." She thought of the huge deed that had dictated her own secret life. *Noble* was not the word for it. *Ignoble*, perhaps. The action that rid Clemmie of her stalker was as long ago as Muffin's good deed. Clemmie rarely thought about what she'd done except in church, when she would walk in feeling almost sinless. But God knew better.

Muffin wilted on Clemmie's sofa, looking old. She *was* old; they both were. There was not a trace of the beautiful girl Tommy Nearing had loved and MacBurton Ward had wanted to find. Clemmie felt the terrible pity that often ran through her when she saw the remnants of beauty. But mostly, she was so tired it hurt. Sunday seemed to have lasted for weeks. And now she had to try to sleep with the venom of the past in her dreams.

Muffin straightened up. "Yes, but now all of a sudden, Helen, MacBurton Ward has taken over the news. He's everywhere. Talk shows, morning shows, podcasts, social media. Trumpeting his year in 'the South.' As if it's a separate country." She slumped down. "Of course, back then, it was."

On the one video clip Clemmie had watched on her phone and in the two articles she'd read, also on her phone, MacBurton Ward had been careful and academic, calmly listing one vile incident after another, although he didn't use the word *incident*. He said *melee, brawl, mental sickness, societal decay*.

On that news clip, a very young TV personality said patronizingly,

"Really, MacBurton, were white people ever lynched? I mean, why would they do that?"

"Because I was a reporter telling it like it was—and what it was, was sickening. Those people had a public history of violence, especially in the nineteen thirties and forties. By the fifties and sixties, it was largely kept offstage, but the violence itself never stopped. It was rampant. And they claimed *I* was incendiary."

He was clearly proud of having been incendiary once. Clemmie wondered if he'd ever been incendiary again. Why had he waited fifty years? Or had he been trying to be heard for fifty years, and suddenly there was a gap in the non-news cycle, and he leaped in?

"The girl who rescued me was young, had long, dark hair, wore a very decorative hat, and drove a large station wagon with fake wood sides. It may have been a Ford Country Squire," he said, as if this were a vital clue.

There had been other faux Woodies then, with the Country Squire among the most popular. But fifty years later, would some ancient, doddering Ferris resident have the slightest idea what car a long-gone neighbor had driven?

"She'll step forward," said MacBurton Ward, nodding confidently into the camera. "There were four would-be killers. I can't prove it, but she can."

"Nice," said the TV guy sarcastically. "You put *her* in mortal danger, while *you're* safely touring for your book."

Do I think Muffin is in *any* danger, let alone mortal? Clemmie asked herself.

MacBurton Ward chuckled. "She's not in danger. They're all old, if they're even alive."

"Old people can still shoot," the host said cheerfully. "Especially in the South."

Muffin Morgan looked across the room at Helen Stephens, in whom she had just confided. *Prissy old maid*, she thought, and squelched this sad summary, but it was true. Helen had never married, never had a man in her life, taught Latin, for heaven's sake, talk about spinstery and useless. She was almost too nice. You knew Helen had never said an ugly thing, used an ugly word, or had an ugly thought. Muffin was surprised they were even friends. She wondered if Helen—in her sweet little life as a sweet little teacher of a dead language to a handful of dweebs—could grasp what it was to be afraid.

My past includes four men willing to kill, thought Muffin. Six if I include Tommy Senior and Ev. Although they're no longer alive. Still. Their influence could be alive. It's *me* MacBurton Ward wants. My story. My identifications. Would one of those remaining men decide to kill the past before Ward stumbles on it?

Old people can still shoot. Especially in the South.

Muffin shuddered and picked up the thread. She was not really telling this story to Helen. She was telling herself.

She had continued north on I-95 that day, swung west on the new interstate, and headed for the little Virginia mountain town where she had graduated from high school. Because a doctor must be paid at the visit, she had had a single check with her that morning, but she'd written it to cash instead, so that Tommy would have no record of money given to an out-of-town doctor. They didn't have a credit card. They'd barely heard of them. Tommy made her keep ten dollars in the glove compartment in case something happened when she was out by herself. She had a few more dollars in her wallet and change purse. She had no other resources.

In Virginia, she took refuge with her great-aunt, her only remaining family. She was a little shaken to find that she mourned as much for her dresses, handbags, and shoes as for her marriage.

Her aunt's attorney suggested that she go to Nevada for six weeks and get a quickie divorce. Her aunt was willing to pay for it. Since Muffin had no clothing with her, she went shopping first. And there in the dress shop she ran into the sister of her old boyfriend John Tee. John Tee—his name was John Theo Morgan, but everybody called him John Tee—had taken her to the sophomore, junior, and senior proms, and she had fully expected him to take her through life. But he joined the Army the day after high school graduation instead of proposing. Muffin met Tommy Nearing during her first and only semester of college, when he came to a dance with Webb, who was going steady with a girl in her dorm. She married Tommy in part because John Tee had kissed her goodbye without a thought.

And here was John Tee again, home from his Army base in Germany on leave. When his sister told him Muffin Revere was in town, he drove to her aunt's, lifted Muffin by the waist into the air, swung her in circles, kissed her mouth and cheeks and throat and hair, and they were in love again in a minute.

She left for Reno. John Tee went back to Germany. Lyndon Johnson got the Civil Rights Bill passed. The Beach Boys' "Get Around" reached number one on the charts. Congress gave President Johnson war powers in some place called Viet Nam. And Muffin Revere, asking for no money, no support, just release, got her divorce.

"I never got in touch with a single person from Ferris," she told Helen. She had been proud of this at the time. She had never called her mother-in-law. Never sent anybody a Christmas or a birthday card. Never used the name Christaphine Nearing again. And most of all, never told her baby's father that he had a son.

———————

Clemmie's heart and soul paused. She too had a son whose existence had been kept from his biological father, but her little boy had been removed from Clemmie's arms. She had held and kissed her baby boy for only a few hours before he was given up for adoption.

Her son and Muffin's must be roughly the same age.

Muffin was in full confession mode, but Clemmie would never reciprocate. She pressed a tissue to her eyes to hide her grief.

"You're weeping for me," said Muffin. "Helen, you're so dear."

Not particularly, thought Clemmie.

Muffin's story went on and on. Clemmie listened helplessly.

———————

John Tee didn't care that the natural father of his first child was his bride's first husband. He called his wife Muffin, of course, barely aware that she had another name.

The Army loved paperwork. She filled in every form as Muffin Morgan, skipping the name Christaphine altogether. If anybody were to ask, she planned to giggle and say, 'Oh, I forgot because I never use that name,' but nobody did. At some point, when they were stationed in the United States, she legally changed her first name to Muffin.

She and John Tee called their little son Robert, and later they had another child, Mary. John Tee stayed in the Army and they lived all over the world and the States, and never had a house of their own, and Muffin didn't care. She'd had a house of her own once, and it hadn't ended well.

Muffin cut off her story. There were memories best not shared, especially with a saint-type person like Helen. But how sharp and painful these unspoken memories were.

A few decades after she fled that oak tree, Martin Luther King Day was established. Muffin was watching a parade on the news and had an awful thought: *Would I would have made that crazy drive down that awful lane and ended my marriage to save a colored man?*

No.

Never.

It had been such brutal, sobering knowledge of her soul.

She buried it. Now she'd have to bury it again. She had a brief, awful vision of Gale, her only Black acquaintance, seeing into her heart and learning what kind of woman Muffin really was. Then she got a grip on herself and breezed through the rest of her bio for Helen's sake, since Helen was so invested, tearful at every turn.

So fast it was like her flight from Tommy, Robert grew up and he too joined the Army. He married another Army brat he met when the family was stationed in Guam, and he and Dinah also lived all over the country and the world. They decided against children because they were having too much fun as a couple. When Robert retired from the Army, he and Dinah chose Southern California because of its glorious beaches and perfect weather.

Mary became a math teacher, married another math teacher, and lived way out on Long Island. They too decided against having children, since they had them all day long in school.

And then John Tee had a heart attack and Muffin was alone, her children thousands of miles apart and no grandchildren.

One day, she drove south to see what a Sun City was like, and what it was like was perfect and Muffin bought her first home. She loved her little villa, which shared a wall with a matching villa. She loved her neighbors and her activities and her new friends. She tried several churches, but they were too big or too small, too

liberal or too conservative, played too much music or played it badly. She decided to try one more: the church Helen liked. Trinity Hill. And there, she explained to Helen, sat her past, one aisle and a few pews away.

NINE

Clemmie was light-headed from the tragic parallel between her life and Muffin's. "So this morning, in church," she said, trying to wrap up, trying to get Muffin out the door, "you believe you saw Haven."

"It was definitely Haven."

"Have you seen him in the last half century?"

"No. But when I was in Ferris, he came home from his freshman year at college on weekends and now and then he hung out with Tommy. There's no doubt in my mind. It was Haven."

Clemmie had never been to one of her own college reunions, because she had faked her college graduation. She never went to a high school reunion because Clementine Lakefield no longer existed. But she had helped organize reunions at schools where she taught. Without name tags and photographs, nobody could recognize anybody.

Oh, they claimed otherwise. "You look exactly the same!" they chorused.

But no one did. Balding heads or dyed hair, glasses or contacts, double chins and wrinkles and brown spots changed people radically. The real punch was weight gain. Add fifty or seventy-five pounds, which many did, and the girl who had once been so flirty and cute or the cool boy most likely to succeed was gone.

If the man in the black SUV or his passenger at that fender bender had raced out of church to look for Muffin, they'd have seen Clemmie instead, with her Snow White looks and bee-stung lips. She could not be confused with bony, angular Christaphine.

True, Clemmie had been wearing the same indigo jacket that Muffin had had on. Perhaps that had registered. If indeed it was Haven. If he had seen Muffin at all. If he even noticed clothing, which the men of her acquaintance did not.

"Even if you're right," she said, unable to stifle a yawn, "and even if he knew you, resurrecting the lynching is the last thing Haven would want. He surely knows you aren't going to talk to MacBurton Ward. Why did we have to run out of the church?"

"I might be seeking the spotlight," snapped Muffin. "I might want to go on a talk show. I might want to reveal Tommy and his family and friends as the awful people they were then."

As a teacher, Clemmie had watched the metamorphosis of many a young jerk. Part of youth was that you were stupid and unthinking. Most boys and girls grew up to understand themselves and the world

better, and they behaved better. But the decision to lynch someone was off any chart Clemmie knew. "Were they really awful people?" she asked. "Or were they average people at an awful time? Maybe they look back with gratitude because Christaphine saved them from an irrevocable crime. Maybe they've spent their lives trying to atone for even thinking the things they thought."

Muffin nodded. "It's what I've told myself over the years. If I ever thought about it. Which I didn't. But there's another problem, Helen. All of those men have children and grandchildren. They would never want their sons or daughters or grandchildren to know about their beliefs and actions in the sixties. They would never want their colleagues and people who respect them and people in their church to know."

"Muffin, how would anybody know? If you're not going to tell and Haven's not going to tell, and surely Tommy won't tell, it'll stay secret."

"Tommy's dead. I looked him up online. The old Ferris paper folded ages ago but the obituaries are still available. Tommy had a heart attack on the golf course twenty years ago. It's sickening, but I felt kind of triumphant that I outlived him. I couldn't find Haven, I can't remember Webb's last name, and Daniel I think was a Smith and there are too many Smiths to try."

"What about your in-laws?"

"Tommy Senior lived into the late nineteen eighties, so he saw every single thing he dreaded come true. There's no way to tell how

he behaved but he kept being chair of this and president of that. Eleanor stepped up, though. She started ESL tutoring in Ferris; she arranged Black History weeks. This from a woman who talked about stoning children as if it was no different from deadheading flowers. Anyway, she died in the eighties too."

"Did Tommy remarry?"

"Yes. They had four children. The obituary listed them. They're married and have children of their own. They shouldn't have to learn that Tommy was one of those four killers. I owe that to Tommy. I took his firstborn son away from him. I have to protect Tommy's other children from the truth."

Clemmie had never once considered the possibility that she owed her rapist a thing. It was her dear son she owed; she had owed him the safety of good parents who could give him a good shot at a good life. And to ensure that, she too had resolved to protect her child from knowledge.

"MacBurton Ward is searching," said Muffin. "If Haven can find me, so can Ward. Ferris was a small town. Everybody knew everybody. They were all intertwined through church and Rotary and Chamber of Commerce and Garden Club. Anybody could deduce that the beautiful young woman with long, dark hair was the wife of Tommy Nearing. Especially since I was never seen again."

Just because people lived in small towns didn't mean they knew each other at all, let alone intimately. They went to different churches, or weren't members of Rotary, or didn't garden. Clemmie

didn't believe that decades later, anybody would remember which wife left which marriage in the summer of 1964.

Tommy wouldn't have made a public announcement. News of his failed marriage would have oozed out eventually, but after all these years, twenty of which Tommy himself had been dead, who would remember that he'd *had* a first marriage, let alone what year?

It was ludicrous and narcissistic to think that people in Ferris had been sitting around for decades waiting to identify Christaphine.

"Think of having to be on talk shows!" cried Muffin, yanking her ponytail in and out of its scrunchie.

Clemmie's patience ebbed. "Enough drama, Muffin. Nobody *has* to be on a talk show. What you are is an elderly retired woman, and that makes you invisible."

"I'm not invisible. Haven found me. And don't use the word 'elderly.' I hate it."

"He didn't *find* you. He *noticed* you. He probably wanted to talk about the old days. You were friends."

Muffin looked from one corner of the little living room to the other as if Haven or Webb or Tommy or Daniel were listening in. She lowered her voice. *"Helen, I think they would kill me to keep me from talking."*

How absurd this is, thought Clemmie. Two old ladies cosseted in a gated community, one of them predicting her own murder over an event from fifty years ago that *didn't happen.*

MONDAY

TEN

Muffin slept poorly. She was awake before dawn. Sunrise wasn't for another hour, but there was sufficient light from the streetlamps for running. Muffin's problems were usually minor and running gave her ease. She reminded herself that people like Susie Kennett with that druggie daughter and the psycho boyfriend had *real* problems.

It was only forty-eight degrees out. She was tired of cold weather. April in South Carolina should be warm. Or hot. Some years, South Carolina had no spring at all but rushed straight into a blazing, oppressive summer. She put on a long-sleeved tee and zipped up her favorite L.L.Bean jacket.

The sidewalk had tilts and cracks so she usually ran in the golf-cart lane on the smooth asphalt, facing traffic. If a golf cart appeared at this hour—very unlikely—she could shift onto the grass.

Once upon a time, she really had run five or six miles a day, but

now she was satisfied with three, and one of those would be a walk. The other two would be more of a slow jog.

Few people in Sun City had reason to get up early, although exercise die-hards would be standing at the doors waiting for the fitness center to open. She had the road to herself.

Helen, who had been so understanding at first, had turned skeptical. But this morning, Muffin couldn't believe her own story either. How could that reporter have gotten her car door open and managed to get in and close it behind him, all while she was slewing around and bumping over ruts and accelerating in the dust? Why hadn't the boys just grabbed him before he reached the car? Why hadn't she crashed in that wild drive at that ridiculous speed? Why hadn't she called her husband when she found herself at the interstate?

Had she exaggerated the truth, or even fabricated parts of it, to match the reporter's narrative?

And why was she so fearful of exposure? Well, of course, she knew why. But that was too awful to think about even in the deepest recesses of her mind.

A large, dark car appeared down the road, coming her way. Helen had described just such a vehicle pausing at the accident Muffin had not even seen, because she'd been lying down in the back seat of Helen's car. She'd been furious at Helen for getting involved, terrified because Haven Nearing had trespassed in her world.

Now she thought, Helen's right. I trespassed in *his* world. It's *his* church. I was the visitor.

The black car was coming very fast. She knew perfectly well that with nobody else on the road, the driver was simply not bothering with the annoying 25 mile-an-hour speed limit. This was not Haven Nearing driving around Sun City before dawn on the off chance he'd spot the former Christaphine Nearing.

Still. It spooked her.

She left the road and ran down a golf-cart path, although it was risky in the dark. This path dipped and wandered, crossing tiny brooks on slatted wooden bridges. She took off her baseball cap, shook her long hair violently, yanked it tight, thrust it through the hole in the back of the cap, and settled the cap back down on her head. Ponytail play was a nervous habit she probably ought to break, but why, exactly? Who cared?

She thought of Tommy and Haven, Daniel and Webb.

The decades never really vanish, she thought. They wait, bulging with our mistakes and misdeeds.

———————

Clemmie opened the glass slider to her little screened porch. The birds were not yet at the feeder. It was just Clemmie and the silent trees. Monday lay soft and empty for her to fill or ignore while she read and dawdled and watched the birds.

Last week, she and her students had held their Latin banquet. The boys wore white sheets for their togas and the principal, taken aback, murmured to her, "Just be sure they don't look like the KKK.

Maybe wear laurels or something so nobody gets the wrong idea. Videos these days can twist anything."

How dreadful if she and her dear students were to end up at the center of some hate investigation. It was perhaps what Muffin feared, and Clemmie had not backed her up.

She went inside, not proud of herself, and saw that Muffin had left her Bible behind. It lay on the coffee table, the little leather suitcase blending into the stacks of books. She would take it over to Muffin later.

Clemmie poured herself coffee. When had the change come from cup and saucer to mug? It was like so many mysterious changes. When did men stop wearing hats? Whatever happened to girdles? Why did you still call it a cup even though it was a mug?

She pondered Muffin's story.

In nineteen sixty-four, when women's lib had yet to launch, a wife really did promise to obey. Did Clemmie believe that a very young bride would abandon her marriage so dramatically and catastrophically? Especially when she was about to have a child? When she had virtually no money?

Clemmie could imagine some difficult phone calls after Christaphine's destruction of the lynching plans, but given the baby, wouldn't Tommy have to shrug and let it go? Of course, they'd have been in a different marriage then—the "obey" section would be off the table. But Muffin had not made that choice. She had leaped into another marriage and left the country.

Clemmie believed in second chances, in forgiveness. If the day ever came when she faced *her* real family, she certainly hoped they would forgive her.

But a man willing to hang a stranger by the neck because the stranger published difficult statements on difficult topics—could such a man ever be dealt with? Wouldn't he always pose a danger to his wife and to others?

Then again, Christaphine's initial guess had been that her husband and his buddies just wanted to scare MacBurton Ward. In that case, the almost lynching would have been cruel and twisted, but not murder. Except that pumped-up young men, goaded and, in fact, ordered to kill... Would they have been *able* to back off?

Clemmie needed something less grotesque to think about. She tapped the *Charlotte Observer* icon on her phone to check the local (usually comfortingly dull) headlines.

MacBurton Ward was a feature story because a source had stepped forward. The unnamed individual and Ward would appear this morning on a local TV talk show.

Who could the source be? A family member? What family member of what generation of which family would ever open that particular door?

Her landline rang. Clemmie gave that to people who needed her number—the plumber, the pharmacy—but who were basically strangers.

It was Wendy Harroll, chair of the funeral committee at Trinity

Hill. They put on receptions during calling hours or after a funeral service, providing pimiento cheese sandwiches cut in triangles, ham biscuits, cookies, crackers and cheese, and sweet or unsweet tea. Clemmie loved working side by side with the other volunteers in the big church kitchen. "Hello, Wendy," she said. She remembered when caller ID was first invented, when you and the caller were both so startled that the other person knew who you were.

"Hi, Helen. We've had a death, an elderly man who was quite a mover and shaker in this area years ago. His bio is amazing, there's nothing he didn't do, so there'll be a lot of people at calling hours, which the family announced would be in Fellowship Hall from four to six today and didn't even ask us first. I'm a little frantic. I found people to set up the tables, put on the tablecloths, and bring out the vase collection. I'm bringing flowers from my garden, so we'll have nice centerpieces. I need somebody to make sandwiches."

"Of course. And I can also work the reception." Clemmie had meant to do nothing much all day, but now she wanted the hustle and bustle, the pleasure of doing something nice for strangers, the chattering with the other church ladies.

"Thank you so much! Can you be there at three thirty? And will you also make the cookie calls? I'll email you the list of women who have made their cookies already and have them in the freezer."

It was tempting to say that making sandwiches was enough, and Wendy should assign cookie calls to somebody else, but Wendy was the chair, and Clemmie's rule in life was, Never be the chair, with its

corollary, Never complain or you might end up as the chair after all. "I will," she said, taking bread out of the freezer.

She filled a large pot with cold water, added eggs, and turned up the heat.

Wendy's email arrived. Clemmie didn't know a single woman on the cookie list. It was a little early to call, but given the time crunch, she couldn't wait long.

Clemmie browsed on her laptop. In what was probably a betrayal of friendship, she wanted verification of Muffin's story.

First she located the obituaries for Tommy's father, Tommy Nearing Senior, and his uncle, Haven's father Ev, who turned out to be Everett. The Nearing brothers were portrayed as outstanding citizens who joined everything, ran everything, and got their pictures in the paper for everything. There were long paragraphs about fundraising for the new hospital wing, being president of Rotary, serving on the school board. She was glad because it meant that they, like most of the South, had bitten the bullet and proceeded to do their best for their towns instead of their worst. On the other hand, perhaps they owned the paper and dictated their public faces.

Clemmie lost interest looking up people she'd never known and thankfully never would. It occurred to her that like Muffin, she had let the decades roll by without asking herself what had happened to the players in her own personal melodrama.

ELEVEN

Clementine Lakefield had spent years hiding from a stalker. Her first line of defense had been to use the name and social security number of a girl in her elementary school who died very young.

Clemmie could barely remember the real Helen, although she had been thankful to Helen every day of her life.

Think of the real Helen's poor parents. Losing their little girl when she was only nine. The empty, endless sorrow as other people's daughters grew up and became women, while their daughter was forever in her grave. How profoundly awful if they had ever found out that Helen's little playmate had been masquerading as Helen all these decades.

But the Stephens family could never have known about Clementine Lakefield's choice of identity.

She clicked on the Connecticut newspaper that covered the

eastern shoreline and opened the obituary section. In the last few decades, online security protections often required your mother's maiden name. Dozens of times, as if she had squatter's rights, Clemmie had entered Helen's mother's name: Coralie Pitkethly Stephens, a name she knew from Helen's ancient passport and birth certificate, which by chance had been sitting at Clemmie's awaiting completion of a school assignment. But Helen died and the papers stayed where they were, year after year, until Clemmie realized that a new identity would save her from her stalker.

Coralie Pitkethly Stephens had died decades ago. Her ashes were buried in the churchyard of the English village in which she had been born.

It sounded so Miss Marple, so sort of tidy.

But what was tidy about outliving your only child?

Clemmie had not outlived her only child. Instead, she had lived her life without him. But Facebook! Blessed Facebook. She had found him there. He had been adopted by loving parents and now was a loving parent himself, and she relied on her daily dose of Facebook to see what his children—her grandchildren!—were doing. As far as she could tell, they were majoring in selfies.

The real Helen's father, John Edmund Stephens, also came up immediately.

Amazingly, he had died only a few months ago at the age of ninety-eight. He had never moved from the house in which he and Coralie had lived with their little girl, Helen. How heartbreaking!

Name, address, and date of death was all the paper provided about John Edmund Stephens. Newspapers had fallen on hard times and now charged for what had once been free. Submitting a long obituary was expensive, aside from the fact that John Edmund Stephens had no children or grandchildren to write it. Obituaries and photographs, videos and condolence messages were usually found now on funeral home sites, on Facebook, or at Legacy.com.

The kitchen timer rang.

Clemmie set the hard-boiled eggs on the counter to cool. Then she started her cookie calls. It was good she didn't know these women because they were uniformly unhappy to have a call this early. On the other hand, they all agreed to drop off their cookies at Fellowship Hall before three thirty.

Clemmie returned to her computer screen.

On Facebook, she occasionally looked up Friends of the Shoreline, which chiefly featured photographs of beaches and sunsets, but also carried tidbits of news from her old hometown. There might be a school closing-for-snow announcement, a homeowner looking for somebody to do a dump run, or a club putting on a fundraiser. Perhaps she would find a mention of Mr. Stephens, citing the funeral home or church where the service had been held. She scrolled toward the date of his death.

Incredibly, there was an ongoing thread about John Edmund Stephens.

Enough people knew a ninety-eight-year-old to post about him?

He must have done wonderful things, like the gentleman whose calling hours were today at Trinity Hill.

No.

The law firm handling his estate had discovered that although his only child, Helen, had been dead for over sixty years, her social security number was active. It had been in use most of that time—a half century of identity theft.

No, no! thought Clemmie.

How had the law firm found out? Could they locate her? What would they do?

She felt so much anxiety that she seemed to float above and around the screen. She could hardly read the posts.

> ...Creepy!
>
> ...I didn't think there even *was* identity theft way back then.
>
> ...Is it a felony? Did the person steal a fortune?
>
> ...No, because the real Helen had no money and the fake Helen never attempted to get any. It must be somebody who needed another identity, not somebody trying to steal.
>
> ...More likely, knowing Social Security as I do—someday I'll tell you what I've been through with those miserable people—it's a glitch. Some innocent person is going to get blamed for SS's failures and stupidity.

...What law firm?

...Curtin, Fiumara, and Bloch.

...How do you know about this identity theft? Do you work for them? Isn't this breach of something? Aren't you supposed to keep stuff confidential?

...I've also had bad experiences with Social Security. I bet the poor other Helen Stephens doesn't even know she's using the wrong numbers. And she's old herself. She has to be. You don't need your SS # until you're working, so fifty years of using it plus twenty years before you start working is seventy so, like, whatever.

...Could we please not trash government workers? I worked for Medicare for twenty-five years, and I regard myself as a soldier for the people.

...So then you retired at 50 and you're getting their retirement money and working a second job and you'll retire from that and get their retirement money, too, right? Typical gov rip-off.

The dialogue went seriously downhill at this point. The contributors had forgotten Helen Stephens.

Clemmie closed the screen.

She thought of the slow, relentless Social Security Administration, which one day would send her a letter about the real Helen Stephens.

Or send an agent.

Or a warrant.

She had cut Helen up and used her like a paper doll—dancing on with her own life while the true Helen lay in a coffin. *Becoming Helen*, while Helen herself lay in the grave.

Clemmie wet a washcloth in cold water and pressed it over her eyes. After a while, she put on foundation and powder, color and mascara. Used the bright-red lipstick that was her trademark. Chose the black wig, thick with tight, black curls, as if she really could still be the adorable pixie of her youth.

What am I actually afraid of? Admitting that I stole Helen? Losing the respect of others? Being arrested and receiving a prison sentence? Or am I mostly afraid of being fingerprinted? Because that could lead to what else I did. Or is my greatest fear that my beloved baby boy—a fine man now approaching retirement age himself, a man I moved here so I could see him from a distance—will find out who he is?

Muffin must feel this awful about *her* past coming back, thought Clemmie.

I should have been nicer to her.

But that was always the case, wasn't it? You should have been nicer.

TWELVE

Muffin sat on a bench near the green while the sky softened and dawn came. She was positive that it had been Haven in church. She had seen him and he had seen her.

If she could have a nice, safe chat with Haven and then they never crossed paths again and he didn't find out what her name was now or where she lived, she'd do it. She'd like to know what happened after she drove out of Tommy's life.

What had he told his family? How had he gotten out from under the attention a vanished wife would bring? What had her in-laws said and done?

Only ugly lies would have worked. Perhaps Tommy claimed that his wife had run away with some other man. It was almost true. A week later Muffin was in love again, and before long, she'd run all the way to an Army base in Europe. All these years,

she had thought how romantic, how *meant* that was. Her true destiny.

It struck her now as appalling. She had abandoned husband, marriage, house, in-laws…and within a few months was leading an entirely different life with entirely different people, and never looking back. What kind of person never looked back?

She so did not want her maiden name, Revere, or her first married name, Nearing, out in public. Her son, Robert, and daughter, Mary, had no idea that there had been a first marriage. All they knew was that Mom and Dad had been high school sweethearts.

Could Muffin trust Virgie to omit from her golf article the name printed on the Bible? The magazine had a two- or three-month time lag between submission and publication, so if Virgie wrote her ladies' nine-hole article now, it wouldn't be out for a while. And the magazine circulated only here in Sun City, so it wasn't on newsstands. Not that such a thing existed anymore. Not to mention that Virgie was getting a little scattered and with any luck would forget the whole thing.

It was silly to be afraid of the past. She had done a good deed back there in Ferris, Muffin told herself. Saved one life; saved four men from committing evil.

It was a bit surprising that local media was touching Ward's claim. Evil was a great story when it happened in somebody else's backyard. Not so much when it's in your own backyard. But the Carolinas were so prosperous, cheerful, and pleasant these days. She

was willing to bet that the media wouldn't drag up, for example, the true shocking, tragic story of Black Army sergeant Isaac Woodard. While wearing his uniform, proof of his service, the poor young man had been attacked and blinded by the police chief of Batesburg, South Carolina, in a fit of rage against an "uppity" black man. It was in part the Woodard horror that convinced Harry Truman to integrate the U.S. armed services in 1948. There were grim segregation events for years to come, but after that people covered their tracks better.

But the tracks in Ferris would lead to Muffin herself. She didn't want to be involved. She didn't want to be questioned.

Muffin could not remember the name of the boy her father-in-law had destroyed. When had that happened? Altogether she had lived in Ferris less than a year and a half, so it must have been in 1963. It was not unlike the Woodard case. The boy had been working for Tommy Senior, repairing an outbuilding. Jubilant about his college acceptance to a good school up north—the first in his family to finish high school, never mind enter college—he'd been dancing around, grinning from ear to ear, bragging about his future.

Tommy Senior felt it was uppity. He lost his temper, jerked the hammer out of the kid's hand, and slammed him in the head with it.

Muffin hadn't been there. She did know that Tommy and Haven had been made to deal with the body.

Nobody had scrubbed the blood off the hammer. Might as well hang it back up on the pegboard and enjoy it.

It had horrified her, but she hadn't said a word. Hadn't done a thing.

The boy's family probably never knew why he didn't show up again, although they would have known for whom he'd been working. They couldn't have gone to the police, who would have shrugged and done nothing, saying that black boys were unreliable, apt to wander off.

MacBurton Ward was right. The truth should be sought. But then Tommy's descendants would learn from television that they had a father, a grandfather, and a great-uncle who had all been violent segregationists. And what about her own son, Robert? Would he find out that he was related to that family? She and Robert were distant already in miles and heart. What if she lost him altogether? Robert communicated so rarely. She had to beg for attention. People here asked why she hadn't retired to San Diego—close to her son and perfect weather. She couldn't admit that she wouldn't have seen any more of him living close by than she did now.

O, Truth! Why did anybody want it?

Muffin finally walked back out to the road. The black car and the dark sky were long gone. She trudged the final mile to White Lily, her own cul-de-sac, but didn't go in. She went on to Blue Lilac. She wanted to thrash everything out with somebody, and the only possible person was Helen. She rang the bell.

The door opened immediately. "Come on in, Muffin," said Helen. "I have the television on. MacBurton Ward is about to be introduced. He's found a source to back him up."

Muffin almost fainted. How could he have found a source? Who could it possibly be?

The man had to be lying. He had talked his way into another minute on TV with some stretched truth that he couldn't substantiate.

Muffin normally loved Helen's living room, which was bright with color and sun, the walls hung with high-school-student art Helen had acquired over the decades, and books everywhere.

But since Helen was primarily a reader, her television was small and did not occupy a prime space in her living room. Muffin considered this arrogant. *I don't waste my time on simpleminded entertainment the way you do; I read Latin.*

Muffin hiked a chair close enough to see the pitiful screen.

MacBurton Ward sat to the left of a young and beautiful white presenter, with the shoulder-length, slightly turned-under blond hair and the Miss America smile required of newswomen these days. Muffin would believe in equality only when female anchors were overweight and plain. On the other hand, news today was entertainment, not journalism, so looks and charm did come first.

The presenter's name was not given, perhaps in the belief that she was too famous to need introductions. It was a local show, though. How famous could she be?

"Good morning, Aprille," said Ward cheerfully.

Aprille. Muffin hated her already.

An elderly Black woman sat on Aprille's right. She was heavyset, with graying hair under a gleaming hat, as if she had just come from

church. She sat bolt upright on the comfy interview armchair. It was difficult to read her expression.

"Good morning!" enthused Aprille. "We're honored to have Miz Stefanie Fortress with us!" Aprille was too busy beaming at the camera to glance at either guest.

Ms. Fortress seemed to correct the pronunciation of her name, but Muffin couldn't quite hear. It didn't look as if Aprille understood either or, for that matter, cared. Ms. Fortress picked up a pad of paper lying on the pretend coffee table of the pretend living room and printed out her name. The camera zoomed in.

ROSE SEFFANIE FORTRESS.

Stefanie! The colored cook her in-laws had shared with her.

Muffin would never have recognized her. She'd been slim and pretty back then, sort of pouty, hovering just this side of inso-lence. Muffin hadn't liked Stefanie one bit. The girl refused to teach her to cook and disliked having her in the kitchen at all, as if it were her kitchen, not Muffin's. She was always singing gospel hymns just when you wanted your own music and not hers. She kept a King James Bible open on the kitchen table, a pane of glass over the pages to keep them clean, and she read aloud, chapter after chapter, in a voice as rich and flowing as the Elizabethan words.

But she didn't talk that way. She talked the way Muffin heard all Black people talk then, leaving out verbs and skipping plurals.

She remembered laughing at Stefanie once, pointing out that

the girl misspelled her own name. "It my name, though," the help had said quietly, eyes down, "so it ain't misspelled."

Muffin would have been within her rights to smack her. But she hadn't. Instead, pointedly, she continued to call her Stefanie.

Now she was filled with shame, but then—as her mother-in-law carefully instructed—you had to keep them in their place. They needed a constant stream of reminders. Like reinforcement in dog training, Mother Eleanor explained.

Muffin stared at the Stefanie sitting in the television studio. It had never crossed her mind to think about the help, then or now.

Thirteen

Clemmie struggled to give Rose Seffanie her attention.

All she could really think about was that a law firm in Connecticut knew that a fake Helen Stephens was out there. The IRS could connect the dots, should they choose. She was a dot. That was her significance after all these years. A dot.

"Miz Fortress is a manager at her local Belk's department store and a deacon in her church," said Aprille. "Stefanie, I understand you lived in Ferris in 1964." Aprille shook her head incredulously, 1964 as remote to her as 1066.

The Black woman held up her scratch pad. "Rose Seffanie," she said clearly. "The esses come together, more like Ro'Seffanie. When I was he'p for the Nearings, they never say it right neither."

Her southern accent was deep and her words came slowly, each syllable weighted. Clemmie had to concentrate to understand. It was

good to have something to concentrate on other than being arrested for five decades of felony. Was there a statute of limitations on identity theft? Would she be guilty only of the last decade and not the first four?

She should probably call a lawyer and be prepared for the worst, but Clemmie could think of no attorney she would trust with any of it, let alone all of it.

"Tell us about 1964, Stefanie."

"Bad year," said Ro'Seffanie, nodding slowly. "In Mississippi? Those three Freedom Riders? They disappear. One of 'em Black, but nobody talk about him much. They wouldn't never investigate except th'other two were white. Black boys in those days, they disappear now and then, nobody never care."

"And in Ferris," said Aprille, moving right along, "what was happening?" She was perky. They could have been discussing shoes.

"We just waitin'. Integration comin' to schools. Could be bad. But we had hope."

Clemmie could feel that hope, thin and shaky and afraid to surface.

Aprille favored MacBurton Ward with her smile. Her teeth were as big and white as Chiclets. Whatever had happened to Chiclets? The disappearance of her once favorite gum moved onto Clemmie's list of mysteries. "Stefanie, let's greet MacBurton Ward, a former *New York Herald Tribune* reporter who was in Ferris in 1964 and is here with us today."

Somewhat to Clemmie's surprise, MacBurton Ward was a good interviewer and easily took over. He got Ro'Seffanie to describe being help in the early sixties for two families named Nearing.

"You must have been very young when you started work," said Ward.

"Thirteen. Not much school then, you're colored." Ro'Seffanie explained that she had been the cook for Tommy Nearing Senior and Miz Eleanor. When their son, Young Tommy, got married, Ro'Seffanie was required to work in the new household as well, hustling back and forth. She didn't have a car. She had to walk. She didn't get paid more.

Slave labor, thought Clemmie. She glanced at Muffin, who was hugging herself, lips pressed together, hypnotized by the screen. Clemmie murmured the intriguing name to herself. Rose Seffanie. You really did have to compress it and say Ro'Seffanie, just as nobody really said Barbara Ann; they said Barbran.

"Now the wife of Young Tommy. What was her name?"

"No!" moaned Muffin. "Don't!"

"I call her 'Yes, ma'am,'" said Ro'Seffanie, not smiling. "Her mother-in-law, she call her Miss Chrissy."

"Did Miss Chrissy help with the cooking and cleaning?"

"No. She busy learnin' to be like Miz Eleanor. Women's club. Flowers. All that. She young and beautiful, like your story. Long, dark hair," said Ro'Seffanie. "But she not your rescuer. She do what she told by her man and his daddy. She not gonna do what you tell

101

in your story. How she even find those four tryna lynch a man? Four men against one little girl? How she make that work? How she dare? Remember, they all armed."

Clemmie rather enjoyed how Ro'Seffanie used the historical present, a Latin favorite, and omitted verb forms of "to be." Latin loved to omit and condense. It was a difficult concept for first- and second-year students. She wondered what Gale would think of this interview, of Ro'Seffanie, of Ro'Seffanie's employers.

"And they a rough family. Tommy Senior, he a bad man, goin' back a lotta bad years, and his daddy before him. Seem impossible now, but they like to beat on Black boys." Her strong voice dwindled and her dignified posture sagged. "Killed some," said Ro'Seffanie softly. "Just play for them."

Twice in one minute, Ro'Seffanie had stated that Tommy Nearing Senior killed Black boys. Neither Aprille nor MacBurton Ward followed up. Clemmie thought, as she often did, that there was something essentially amoral about reporters. Because nobody cared about those dead Black boys now either.

To Clemmie, it was incontrovertible proof that Ward was chasing his "lynching" to increase his book sales. Not that he'd finished writing his book, let alone published it. He was missing a crucial chapter. It didn't sound as if Ro'Seffanie could supply what he needed.

But she had stated the Nearing name out loud. If Tommy's children and grandchildren still lived in the Carolinas, or even if they didn't, they knew now or would shortly learn what the Nearing men

had been. Clemmie suspected that the Nearings would not only deny it, but get away with the denial.

Her cell phone rang. She picked up because it was a local number and possibly a cookie lady. "Hello?" she said, getting to her feet, heading out of the room so she wouldn't disturb Muffin. But hadn't she used the landline for the cookie ladies? They wouldn't have her cell number.

It was a woman's voice, low and urgent. "Using information in the federal database, the Internal Revenue Service is filing a lawsuit against you. An arrest warrant has been issued in your name."

Clemmie gasped. *They were already acting. They had already found her.*

"An agent is waiting for you to call," rasped the voice.

I'm having a heart attack, thought Clemmie, while Muffin is glued to the television.

Then she came to her senses. An agent would not be waiting for Clemmie to call back. This was a scam. A robocall.

Clemmie managed to poke the right buttons to block future calls, but she could not disconnect her racing heart. It's nothing, she said to herself. That call went to a million other people at the same time it went to me. It has no meaning.

But someday it will.

On television, MacBurton Ward asked, "Miss Chrissy leaves the marriage in 1964, is that right?"

"Nobody know," said Ro'Seffanie. "Mister Tommy, that's Tommy

Senior, one day he tell me I just workin' for him now. So I don't go back to Young Tommy's house. But that summer, see, they find the bodies of the Freedom Riders in Mississippi. Buried in a dirt dam that made a pond at a farm. After that, nobody talk about nothin' else. White, Black. It the only topic. A long time before you start thinking—where Miss Chrissy at anyway?"

FOURTEEN

Daniel had retired after many hard years working for a corporation that sent him all over America. The moment he and Virgie toured Sun City, he knew this was his destiny. All that golf. He played most days of the week, usually in Sun City, but often elsewhere; the Charlotte area was packed with golf courses. When he couldn't play golf because of weather, he went to the clubhouse for pool and poker.

His wife was a superior cook, but Virgie had tired of cooking. They generally ate out, but Daniel liked breakfast at home. He wanted his coffee, flavored creamers, and orange juice, his toast and eggs and grits. He made it himself these days and sat at the breakfast bar, watching the morning news.

You got attached to your particular morning show. He liked the tall, willowy blond with the great hair and the empty head. Aprille delighted in crossing her legs and adjusting her skirt. You never saw

skirts anymore, but this girl had a new one every day. She couldn't conduct an interview very well. Her job was to appreciate other people's remarks, and she was superior at nodding and beaming.

MacBurton Ward had gotten himself on again. It kind of worried Daniel but not really. If the man had had any way to get the names of the four boys, he'd've printed the story years ago.

And then, out of a long ago that was *so* long ago Daniel had forgotten it, here was Tommy Senior and Eleanor Nearing's help. Seffanie. Christaphine had always said it with the *t* it didn't have: Stefanie. Since help couldn't correct the missus, Seffanie had to let it go. She couldn't risk Tommy Senior or Ev knowing she'd talked back. The Nearing men were proud of their hot tempers. And what was the point in cherishing your hot temper if you didn't follow up with a little action? Let some colored get into an argument with Ev Nearing, when back then, colored weren't allowed to argue, and they'd get beaten to pieces.

Daniel hated remembering this stuff. He hated remembering that all those decades ago, when it was actually happening, he didn't notice. It was just how you lived; how it was. His own family had been nice. He still believed that, partly because his parents had been relieved when his friendship with the Nearing boys faded away. They were a bad influence, his mother said.

For sure, he thought now.

Virgie sat next to him. She was a nonstop talker and no TV show ever slowed her down. This made her an asset in any gathering

because there could never be silence or awkwardness. But it was tough to follow the Ward interview with her talking over it.

Right now Virgie was full of her Bible study group. "Muffin? You know Muffin Morgan? She lives down on White Lily? Y'all will never guess her real name."

Daniel remembered meeting Muffin only because it was such a silly name for a woman over seventy. He thought maybe they'd played bocce against her team. If that had been Muffin, she was thin, almost gaunt, with deep facial crevices and long hair she seemed to think was attractive because she tossed it around as if she were still a cheerleader and adorable.

Daniel chastised himself. It wasn't as if he and Virgie were still good-looking. Listen, you eat Virgie's cooking for your whole adult life, you're going to have a serious belly and several chins. As for hair, at least Muffin had some.

Seffanie was saying, "They a rough family. Tommy Senior, he a bad man, going back many bad years, and his daddy before him. You don't believe it now, seem impossible now, but they like to beat on Black boys. Killed some. Nobody care, not then. Just play for them."

Always doing their civic duty, Daniel remembered, serving on boards, chairing committees. A subset of their credo was: Never let coloreds get out of line. Arson and whipping had been in that family for generations. The Nearings had been stunned when desegregation really did threaten Ferris. They hated the outside agitators, stirring

up perfectly good colored and giving them ideas. Not that Tommy Senior or Ev thought there were good ones. There were just less worthless ones.

Funny, but you forgot about the help. You didn't notice them when they were there, and over the passage of years, you forgot there had been any. Could Seffanie actually know something? Daniel imagined every single person in Sun City finding out that he had once come close to hanging a man.

He looked at his wife, sweet, babbling Virgie, who had pretty much loved him all these years and forgiven his many trespasses. He didn't want to hurt her.

———

Muffin clenched her jaw to keep her teeth from chattering.

MacBurton Ward wanted to know the name of Young Tommy's wife, which meant that he had a glimmer of the truth. Or he already possessed the truth but wanted Stefanie to say it.

I call her 'Yes, ma'am,' Stefanie had said. *Her mother-in-law, she call her Miss Chrissy.*

But if Stefanie remembers me at all, she remembers my real name, thought Muffin. Christaphine is the only thing Tommy called me. And since the only thing MacBurton Ward wants is my name, so I can tell him who the lynch party was, why is Stefanie on this show at all, except to identify me?

The interview was wrapping up. Stefanie was now looking

straight into the camera. Straight at Muffin, as if she too was looking for Christaphine Nearing.

Muffin looked away, only to see her own face reflected in a mirror on Helen's wall. No makeup. Sweat-drenched hair. Deep, deep wrinkles. She hadn't recognized Stefanie after all these years, and neither could anybody see the Christaphine she had once been.

In fact, she realized, humiliated to her toes, Haven could not have recognized her on Sunday. She wasn't a young beauty. She was a skinny old bag who dyed her hair. He just happened to glance over and she, self-centered as always, assumed it was about her.

On the screen, Stefanie leaned forward, big, straight-backed, and fierce, like a Sunday School teacher delivering the news of hell. Muffin had a faint memory that Stefanie really had been a Sunday School teacher. It was why she refused to work on the seventh day of the week at a time when the refusal of a white man's order was pure danger. The Nearing clan was forced to have Sunday dinner at the K&W Cafeteria or the country club, a basic nine-hole golf course whose dining room served mediocre food.

Stefanie said, "If what you say happen, Mr. Ward, and if she your girl...she dead. Because her men? Those Nearing men? They kill her in a heartbeat, she do a thang like that."

———————

Tommy had never spoken about it, but somehow Daniel and Haven and Webb knew that one summer day, Tommy's daddy had lost his

temper with a yard boy. You didn't mean to kill them but they had thin skulls, and so much going on in the world, you had to watch yourself even though it was your obligation to control those people. Tommy's daddy had ordered Tommy to bury the body. You'd have to do it quick. Flesh rotted fast in the Carolina heat. Maybe toss the body under a tarp in a pickup. In which case, Daniel had ridden in that pickup.

But Tommy was dead. Facts couldn't hurt him. Daniel had had nothing to do with that supposedly typical Nearing event. Daniel's involvement was the following year, 1964, and that—thank God and Christaphine—had had no result. Over the decades, he had managed to gloss over how close they had come to killing a stranger for nothing. Now the pure viciousness of it crept up and around his chest, patting his heart.

We didn't do it, though, he reminded himself, for about the millionth time.

Daniel wondered now if Tommy had coaxed him to help in 1964 because then he *would* be part of it, could never get out from under it.

Gangs today in crime-ridden American cities and cartels in Mexico ordered a young man to prove himself with bloodshed. It had been no different in Ferris. He and Webb and Haven and Tommy had been told to prove their allegiance to a different kind of gang.

Christaphine had shown more guts than the four of them put together.

"It was printed in gold on her Bible," said Virgie. "The prettiest name I ever did hear."

Daniel had no idea what his wife was talking about.

"Muffin's real name," Virgie reminded him. "Christaphine Angelique Revere." Virgie enjoyed the sound of that so much she said it again. "Christaphine Angelique Revere." Then she actually sang it, like a nursery rhyme. *Christaphine Angelique Revere.*

Daniel made an actual decision not to have the heart attack. He swallowed it, held his breath against it, stiffened his ribs to contain it.

"You okay, honey?" asked Virgie.

He smiled. "Big bite. Just have to wash it down."

Tommy's wife *here*? A friend of Virgie's?

And yet Sun City was full of impossible coincidences. Just last week two women bumped into each other at the line dancing club—and thirty years ago, they'd been on the same school board in Norwalk, Connecticut.

If Christaphine is watching this TV interview, he thought, she'll reach out to MacBurton Ward. Get her moment in the sun for her good deed. Bask in the attention of television and Twitter and Facebook.

He would have said that he was safe inside the name Smith. Too many Smiths out there. He never had to change identities; he owned one of the names with a common identity, lost before you began. But Virgie was a talker.

Even if Christaphine—Muffin—chose to lie low, Ro'Seffanie had given out the name Tommy Nearing. It couldn't be that hard for Ward to find out the wife's name. Wouldn't be property records—houses then were exclusively in the husband's name. Not old phone books, because all numbers were under the husband's name too. Marriage records, though. That would probably be quick and easy. MacBurton Ward would broadcast the name Christaphine, Virgie would make the connection to Muffin Morgan, and once Virgie knew, the universe would know.

A heart attack wasn't looking so bad. The grave had its uses. Other people had to deal with what you left behind.

"More coffee?" asked his wife.

"Thanks, honey, I will."

He remembered Tommy's beautiful, sweet wife roaring toward them. Screaming. Leaning on the horn. The station wagon raising huge clouds of dust. The four of them leaping out of her way. *"Don't you even think about being murderers!"* she had yelled, her voice huge and raw and brassy, the exact opposite of who she was. He remembered her shrieking at the reporter, *"Get in the car!"* and speeding out of there like NASCAR, a tornado of dust billowing up behind her.

Daniel had expected Tommy to grab his shotgun from his truck and blow out her tires, but Tommy began laughing. He yanked down his bandanna mask. "Wow! Who knew? She is something! Our kids are gonna be a treat! Damn. I love southern women."

Daniel hadn't believed that for one second. Tommy's pride

was his soul. He'd catch up to the station wagon he had bought for Christaphine and kill them both. Daniel had freed himself from his sheet, balling it up, wondering how and where to get rid of the fabric, how and where to get rid of these friendships.

At the breakfast bar, Virgie was still talking. It seemed that Muffin had begged her not to use that beautiful, unusual name in her magazine article about nine-hole golf.

Did this mean that Muffin wanted to stay hidden? Excellent. "Then I think that would be the courteous thing to do," said Daniel. In his mind's eye, he saw Christaphine's long, dark hair flying out the window of the Ford Country Squire. She had vanished that day with the reporter and never came back.

Tommy was devastated, or so he said. She communicated through a lawyer, who returned Tommy's heartfelt letters. He drove up to Virginia but the aunt's house was locked up and apparently not occupied, the neighbors didn't know anything, and nobody in town seemed to have heard of a person named Christaphine. In the end, he gave up and signed the divorce papers that came in the mail.

Course, he got over it. Married again. Had four great kids. If he ever thought about Christaphine, he didn't say so. But by then you didn't talk about the nineteen sixties anyway. Desegregation happened, and a decade later, you weren't sure what you'd been so worried about. Life got ordinary again, just a different ordinary. As for the mud you'd stumbled in (or created), you looked away. Far away.

On the television, Seffanie spoke in a truly scary voice: deep and

heavy and oozing doom. "If what you say ever happen, Mr. Ward, and if she your girl…she dead."

Daid, Seffanie pronounced it, drawing it out. *Daid*. "Because her men? Those Nearings? They kill her in a heartbeat, she do a thang like that."

Oh my God, thought Daniel Smith. How do I really know that Christaphine got away? How do I know Tommy actually got a divorce? He and his daddy could have—

Then he remembered the Bible with Christaphine's name on it. Christaphine was Muffin Morgan and she lived right here.

How easily he had believed that Tommy would have killed her.

FIFTEEN

Clemmie found Ro'Seffanie's final statement extraordinarily provocative. *She daid.*

What would any living Nearing family member say and do now? The wrath of the Nearings would be powerful. Was Ro'Seffanie safe? Where did she live? Was she still in Ferris? Could she risk going home again? Her grandchildren might even attend school with Nearing grandchildren. How would that go? *Oh, hi, yes, your gramma is accusing our entire family of being homicidal. But we're still friends, right?*

And then the interview was over. MacBurton Ward simply smiled at the camera but Ro'Seffanie looked startled, even upset. She has more to say, thought Clemmie. She didn't know she'd run out of time. She didn't know that Aprille doesn't actually care about her story; Aprille's just filling the morning slot.

Aprille and Rose Seffanie Fortress and MacBurton Ward vanished in the way of television. Ads spurted over the screen, followed by desperate warnings about weather. Clemmie turned off the television. She liked television better anyway when the screen was blank.

Muffin looked shell-shocked.

Clemmie's cell phone rang. A stab of IRS fear went through her and her heart leaped. But she knew this caller, and his problems, in fact, were greater than hers.

"I'm so sorry, Helen, I apologize," said Chip in his creaky, sad voice. "I know I could call one of those car services where they just show up out of nowhere and take you, and then you phone again when you're ready to leave and another driver shows up, but Helen, my back really hurts. Three Tylenol haven't touched it. I don't want to be in the back seat of some stranger's car. I know I've asked you too often, but can you take me up to Memory Care again?"

Clemmie, who had had little of it, honored love. If she could help Chip sit there and love his wife, she would do it.

She sifted through the day's obligations. She could finish fixing the sandwiches, wrap and refrigerate them, take Chip back and forth, come home to collect the sandwiches, and still make it to church on time, but it would be close. "Chip, if I come over shortly and drive you up, can you find somebody else to bring you home?" She turned to Muffin. "Can you pick Chip up?"

Muffin glared at her. "Were you watching that interview, Helen? I have a full plate, thank you. Now not just MacBurton Ward but

the *police* will look for me, because Stefanie told them I've been murdered."

Even now you can't be bothered to say her name correctly, thought Clemmie. A name that matters so much to her, Rose Seffanie printed it out and held it up to the camera.

Clemmie had the oddest feeling that Ro'Seffanie's deep accent had been somewhat of a choice; for whatever reason, Ro'Seffanie had chosen dialect, but she could have spoken quite differently had she thought it best. Ro'Seffanie had a strategy that would probably never be clear to Clemmie, who was a complete outsider. She wondered if maybe holding up the printed name was an act intended for a particular viewer. The vanished Christaphine, perhaps. Or the vanished four young men.

"I've worn out my welcome," said Chip.

Clemmie had forgotten she was even on the phone. She glanced at it, thinking how odd that this slender rectangle was likely to be the conduit for ruining her existence as Helen Stephens. Chip talked on. "Ah, Helen, it's such a mess."

Truly. "If you're willing to stay only one hour," said Clemmie, "I'll drive you both ways."

"I like to feed Millie lunch, though. She can't use a fork or spoon any more. The staff will get to it eventually, but I like to do it. If you'll drive me up, I'll call everybody I've ever met when it's time to go home."

"Twenty minutes then," said Clemmie. She resolved to think of

nothing but Chip and the cookie ladies. She would block her IRS and Social Security worries. Fear was not going to rule at this stage of the game.

The true Helen is dead, she thought, and I'm calling it a game.

Muffin's identity had just been flung into the public domain. Clemmie's identities were soon to be scraped out of paper files and e-files, tax returns and driver's licenses and passports. Then she would see whether identity theft was a game.

"Chip's using you, Helen," said Muffin. "You're too soft."

"He's overwhelmed," said Clemmie. "And I'm not too soft. I'm just the right soft."

Muffin shrugged. "I've got table tennis and water aerobics coming up on my schedule, and I need a shower and I haven't even had breakfast yet. Bye."

How could Muffin shrug after seeing Ro'Seffanie after all these years? After getting a glimmer of what life had been like for the help in the Nearing households? Clemmie had a stab of dislike for her friend. She closed the door behind Muffin.

Beside her, a pile of library books sat on the tiny hall table. Before she borrowed a new novel, Clemmie liked to read its reviews on her phone. If a reviewer said it was a searing examination of the dark underbelly of American society, she put it back on the shelf. There would be nothing heartwarming in such a book, and Clemmie read fiction in order to feel better, not worse.

Because her men? Those Nearings? They kill her in a heartbeat, she do

a thang like that... They both KKK. They like to beat on Black boys. Killed some. Just play for them.

Clemmie had a feeling that the dark underbelly of a Jim Crow world was about to receive a searing examination.

And the dark underbelly of her own life? Was it being examined even now? Was some officer in some IRS building or police station running searches this minute to find the right Helen Stephens?

———————

On the drive up to Memory Care, Chip was eager to chat and Clemmie was eager to be distracted. He began with sports, moved into the staggering amount of commercial development along the previously rural road and segued into church. Chip didn't like going alone to church. "The pew feels so empty. I'd rather just sit at Memory Care with Millie. Although in a way, that's worse, because she's empty too. How can there be a condition where a living person's soul empties away?"

High on the list of unanswerable questions.

Clemmie's plan was to drop Chip off at the front entrance and speed away, but the poor man barely had the strength to open the car door. When at last he had both shoes on the pavement and heaved himself upright, he just stood there, wedged in the triangle of the open door and the seat, his breathing fast and shallow.

"Are you having a heart attack, Chip? Do I call 911?"

"Back pain. Let me stand here a minute."

Clemmie turned off the engine, went inside, got a wheelchair, and brought it out. Chip maneuvered himself around and fell into it with another gasp of pain. He set his jaw and held his breath for a bit.

Chip wasn't a small man. She wasn't strong enough to push the chair up the slight ramp. She had to go back in, find an aide, wait for him to be free, and then they both went back to get Chip, who looked as if he wanted to beat something up. Probably old age. An enemy nobody ever beat.

"I never thought I'd be in a wheelchair," he said to Clemmie, who had the unusual experience of looking down at a tall man.

The aide said cheerfully, "You count your blessings, Mr. Chip. You have such a nice neighbor to help you."

Chip would clearly have preferred to deck somebody than to count blessings. "I was in construction," he said to Clemmie. "I was strong."

"You had lentil soup instead of fried fish," agreed Clemmie.

"Well, no. I'm not insane. Of course fried fish. Hush puppies. Onion rings. But I don't think they give you back problems." He closed his eyes. "Actually, Helen, I can't stay long after all. I didn't bring pain pills with me. Can you stay half an hour and take me home? And then I have to figure out what to do. I can't go on like this."

Sixteen

When she had deposited Chip at his house, Clemmie drove home, loaded up her sandwiches, and drove to church. She shut her mind to the past and walked into Fellowship Hall.

It was a large, plain space used for coffee hour, church suppers, youth group activities, basketball games, rummage sales, and funeral calling hours. The sexton had put up ten round tables. A volunteer was dragging out a blue plastic tub filled with neatly folded white tablecloths, paper goods, and plastic cups. Clemmie carried her first sandwich tray over to the only rectangular table.

"Sandwiches!" cried a chubby woman in a turquoise paisley top with a matching cardigan. "Mmmm! I see pimiento cheese! I see egg salad! You did us proud, honey."

Clemmie was not a paisley fan, but when she considered the judgments shortly to come upon her, perhaps she should not judge a

stranger on the basis of shirt pattern. She smiled at her cheerful new acquaintance. "Thank you. I'll be right back. I have more sandwiches in the car."

"More! What were your marching orders, anyway?"

"Wendy said to bring enough. So I also have ham and tuna."

"My word. All we did was drive here."

"We'll help carry, though," said the blue-bin man, possibly the husband, and the three of them went out to Clemmie's car.

"Brrrr. It's chilly again," said the woman. "But you have the loveliest jacket. Such a great color. I absolutely love blue, and that blue is so deep and rich and striking."

Clemmie brought forth her L.L.Bean shopping story.

"I've always wanted to go there!" cried the woman. "But we've never been to New England. It sounds so—I don't know—Yankee. And where are *you* from, sugar?"

"Sun City," Clemmie said, although she knew the question meant, Where did you move from, since your accent tells me you are not a South Carolinian? But Clemmie never told anybody anything. "How about you?"

"Oh, well, we lived in Austin forever. When it was time to retire, we came back to our Carolina roots. I'm a Low Country girl, but it's so expensive there, plus all the flooding, and we don't have any family left in that area. But we have two kids in Charlotte and some grands. Sun City wasn't built when we moved back or we would have considered it. You people seem to have a great life. Summer camp with good houses."

Clemmie unlocked her car.

The husband took both trays. "You fixed all of this? You are some worker. We didn't even buy paper goods."

"You showed up, though. You still get points. Although not as many as I do."

They were laughing on the way back into the building, and Clemmie felt warm with friendship to come. They set the four sandwich trays at intervals on the long table and the woman said, "Now don't laugh and make jokes, I've heard them all, but my name is Dodo."

"I would never laugh," said Clemmie, "but I'm not sure I can address a perfectly nice, articulate, attractive woman as Dodo."

The man did laugh. "I'm Dodo's husband and I agree, but she likes it. When I call her Dorothy, she says, 'What? Are you mad at me?'"

Dodo was dividing paper napkins into convenient little stacks up and down the table, but the husband had finished his tasks. Clemmie put out her hand. "Helen Stephens."

"Glad to meet you, Helen. Haven Nearing."

———

By four-thirty, people were pouring into Fellowship Hall. They stood in line, chatting with old friends. At the sight of sandwiches, they cried out with pleasure, having come straight from work. But they didn't want to lose their place, so Haven carried sandwich trays

down the line while Dodo handed out paper plates. Clemmie poured tea and ice water, brewed coffee, and refilled the creamers. Her hand didn't shake, as if she routinely worked with people who were in the habit of lynching.

Stop it! she told herself. They didn't hang Ward at all, let alone make a habit of it.

Dodo and Haven made a second pass, with cookies.

The line moved slowly because everybody had stories to tell. There was hugging but no tears. The deceased had had a long life and lived it well.

As always, Clemmie questioned her own life. She'd lived it well, but alone. All this hugging and closeness stabbed her a bit, although after so many years, she should be used to it. She thought about another very old man named John Edmund Stephens.

The sandwiches were gone. The cookie platters were down to crumbs. Clemmie suddenly wanted peanut butter cookies, the kind where you pressed fork tines into the dough for a crisscross pattern. Perhaps she would make a batch tonight. She was in need of a soothing activity.

"Let's sit," said Haven, collapsing at an empty table.

This pleasant, easygoing man was Haven, son of Ev, who broke people's arms when they annoyed him. Cousin to Tommy. One of the four. She didn't want to sit with him, but she also didn't want to offend him, and she did want to know Dodo better. "I'll get a cup of coffee first," she said.

"I want a cup too," said Dodo. "I'll get them both. What do you take?"

And before long, Clemmie was sipping good, strong coffee and telling them about Chip because the real topics on her mind were untouchable.

"Do Chip and Millie have children?" asked Dodo. "Usually the children can coax their father or mother into a safer, easier place. Because Chip will wear out the neighborhood and then what?"

"He's never mentioned a son or daughter. And certainly nobody is helping at the moment."

"That's awful," said Dodo. "We've got five. Two are useless in a crunch and one lives at the end of the world. But the other two we see all the time. So we'd have help if we were in Chip's predicament, which God forbid. Helen, you look wiped out. You've done more than your share. There are only a dozen guests still here. You head on home. Haven and I can hold down the fort."

Clemmie could not resist this unexpected cue. "Fort," she mused. "There was a woman on a TV talk show today whose last name is Fortress. Such an unusual name. Are you following that MacBurton Ward story?"

Immediately she was ashamed. Who was she, with more secrets than anyone, to pry? She didn't want to go deeper in Haven's dark past. Dark pasts, her own, for example, should stay where they belonged. Safely in the shadows. Was that immoral? Probably.

"I guess everybody's following that story," said Dodo. "It's

remarkable that a man can get himself so much publicity over something that didn't happen."

Haven said, "I'll clean up the drinks table." He crossed the room.

Dodo said in the confiding voice of old friends, "Haven grew up in the town that man Ward is talking about. He was never fond of Ferris, but at the same time, he hates hearing anything ugly about it. We visited Ferris now and then over the years, but Haven's father died, his mother moved to the coast to live with her sister, and Haven sold the Ferris house. Ferris is one of those leftover towns now; the main street's all boarded up, the factories and the textile mill closed forever ago." She finished her coffee. "When Haven retired, we wanted to be close to our two children in Charlotte, so we never even drove down to see Ferris."

You weren't on your guard with church family. Dodo obviously felt close to Clemmie already.

"We settled on Cobble Creek," Dodo went on. "There is no creek and no houses are built with cobblestones, so the name makes Haven crazy, but the clubhouse is luxurious and meals are outstanding and our house backs onto Cobble Creek Golf Course, where we play all the time. Do you play, Helen? No, you don't have a minute. You're busy taking care of your neighbors. It's wonderful that you're helping Chip so much, but it's good that Chip realizes he can't go on. He has to take the next step.

"We all dread the next step," she went on. "Haven refused to consider one of those retirement centers where you shift across

the campus into assisted living and from there into memory care and from there into hospice. A long, sad row of brick buildings all mapped out for your downhill slide. He hates assisted-living dining rooms because they have to have a little barn for all the walkers. The years go by and they have to enlarge the barn."

She and Clemmie giggled. "I so understand," said Clemmie. "Especially the misuse of both 'cobble' and 'creek.' Now do your children also attend Trinity Hill? Did I by any chance see you last week with your son?" *Stop it!* she said to herself. *Leave this alone.*

"I wish it were so. Our son, bless his heart—after growing up in church and youth group, achieving Eagle Scout in the troop our church sponsored—decided church is too time-consuming. He needs his Sundays for himself, you see. He and his wife don't even have a church."

So it wasn't their son driving the black SUV the other day, and it couldn't have been Haven in the passenger seat. Muffin had been right that it was Haven in church and wrong that he tried to follow them.

I like Dodo, Clemmie thought. I even like Haven. How can I like a man who once planned a lynching? But then, how could anybody like me if they knew my past? Because I didn't just plan. I acted.

When she was safely home, needing no supper because of nibbling so much funeral food, and entirely lacking the energy to whip up peanut butter cookies, Clemmie gathered her courage.

What really happened to people who committed identity theft?

At the computer, she began exploring.

She turned up a law stating that it was criminal to "knowingly transfer or use, without lawful authority, a means of identification of another person with the intent to commit, or to aid or abet, any unlawful activity."

She had not committed, aided, or abetted any unlawful activity by using Helen Stephens's name. That wouldn't make it legal, but it also did not seem to be a crime.

Another source said there had to be "harm" for the police to get involved. Nothing had harmed the real Helen, who had died more than a decade before Clemmie took her name. It had not harmed the real Helen's family, who never knew. No bills had been sent to or paid by the real Stephens family; no assets taken from them.

She checked the various states in which she had lived and worked as Helen Stephens. Each one specified "criminal intent" as part of the charge in identity theft. Each state had its own definition of identity theft. She was glad she hadn't ever taught school under a fake name in Louisiana, where she could be imprisoned with or without hard labor for not more than ten years.

She found no references to people who used another person's name and social security numbers *without* intent to harm.

She had not stolen the real Helen's papers; Helen had given them to her as part of a school assignment. A court might find that she should have returned those papers to Helen's family. But she had

been in grade school. Would they hold her responsible for failing to correct the situation when she became an adult?

In the search line, she typed: *Does anybody actually go to jail for identity theft?*

The top answer discussed the sad reality that law enforcement had limited resources to investigate and prosecute crimes. What to spend time on? They had to prioritize. Go after somebody who stole information from a mailbox and opened a credit card? Or go after a murderer? Invest weeks tracing a possible online scam? Or go after yet another murderer?

The murderer, said a police source, is always the right choice in that scenario.

This was not, in fact, comforting.

There was a murder in Clementine Lakefield's past.

TUESDAY

SEVENTEEN

Tuesday morning, Muffin could not stay away from the television. She turned on Aprille's show. Stefanie was a guest again, but without MacBurton Ward. Why had the woman been asked back? What else could she have to say?

Muffin wrapped up in a blanket she did not need, cocooning herself against Stefanie's assault.

Aprille began with a question about Tommy Senior. A photograph was produced from some ancient Chamber of Commerce event. Muffin had forgotten how handsome the Nearing men were.

Stefanie nodded. "Mister Tommy, he bad all the way through, but he pretend nice. He smile, he chuckle. He a little handsy, though."

"Handsy?" asked Aprille, as though she could not fathom what this might mean.

"White men back then, they hate Black people, but they like

dark meat. And Young Tommy, he learn everything from his daddy. Maybe that why Miss Chrissy leave. She walk in on him, maybe."

Muffin was furious. That was not true! Tommy had been faithful to her! He had adored her with his whole heart and mind and soul and, for sure, his body. And this horrible, mean woman who knew *nothing* was tossing out ugly gossip with no proof whatsoever.

But what did Muffin know, really? Tommy had had two cars and a truck. He arranged his own work hours. He had the ways and means to go anywhere with anyone.

Fifty years have gone by, she thought, and I'm crushed.

Aprille produced her beautiful smile and said, "Let's—"

Stefanie held up a big, flat hand. "Now we talk about my cousin Micah. My cousin Micah, in 1963, he accepted to college in Ohio, where we got family. Our preacher he'p with the application, 'cause our family, we don't know how. Nobody in our family gone past sixth grade. Although the Bible, we read that front to back, out loud, all our lives. So one thing we know: the Lord. But Micah, *he goin' to college*. Proud? We are so proud, we can't think on nothing else. And he on a job with Mister Tommy Senior, earnin' money for college in the fall. One day, he don't never git seen again. You forget about Miss Chrissy, hear? You forget about this MacBurton Ward. Because they nothin', and anyway, nothin' happen. You find out about my cousin."

Nineteen sixty-three.

Muffin had been madly in love. Practically every thought was about Tommy. The one real flaw was the constant presence of her

in-laws. Either they were at her house or she was at theirs. Mother Eleanor had a full agenda for shaping Tommy's wife.

She'd been vaguely aware that Tommy Senior had a yard boy. Some black kid full of laughter and motion: dancing, cartwheeling, singing to himself.

"See?" her father-in-law said one sultry afternoon on the verandah when she was served lemonade and he mixed himself something way stronger. "They're always happy. We don't need to change schools or anything else in Ferris. They just sing and dance. They're fine the way things are."

But then the yard boy got accepted in some college: some real college, up north.

It was an extraordinary event for a colored from Ferris. The University of Mississippi had desegregated just that year, accompanied by appalling violence. Clemson University had accepted its first black student, Harvey Gantt. State police had to escort him.

The Nearing brothers were beside themselves over these events. Literally. They were standing outside their civilized bodies and their civilized behavior.

They goaded each other. *Give 'em an inch, they take a mile.*

Ruining decent schools and decent people.

Makes me sick.

The yard boy used to sing a little ditty to himself, or maybe to the world. *Go-in to m' coll-ege…ah one two three four…getting me a dee-gree.*

Oh, Lord, thought Muffin.

The yard boy must have been Stefanie's cousin Micah.

And this was why Stefanie had wanted to be on Aprille's program: to talk about the killing of Micah. A killing Christaphine had known about and shrugged about because that was how things were.

And now that would also come out: Muffin Morgan, once Christaphine Nearing, was part of a family that murdered a teenager without a tremor.

Haven had watched the morning news ever since he retired. Long, slow breakfasts, Dodo puttering around, Haven flipping through a newspaper almost too thin to bother with. He couldn't stand to watch the local news again today. But if he didn't, worry about what he'd missed would chew on his guts. You didn't hear about ulcers anymore. Maybe there was an ulcer pill. If he heard one more thing about Ferris, he was going to get an ulcer.

His own father had died from a perforated ulcer. Haven had been amazed that Everett Nearing had enough conscience to feel stress, let alone die from it. After his mother passed, Haven had sold the house in Ferris. That was what? Twenty-five years ago? Thirty? He assumed it was still a failed town, but if you went by the exuberant growth in and around Charlotte, spreading down into South Carolina, taking over another village or two every year, maybe even Ferris had come into the money. Maybe people were actually commuting somewhere from Ferris. Building mega mansions.

On his cell, he entered "Ferris, SC." He clicked images. Ferris had become a city! He went to real estate ads. Not a cheap city either. No trace on the map of his old high school or the old colored school. Subdivisions like self-contained spiderwebs clotted the old farmland. The present high school was a vast campus miles from the old center of town.

On the television screen, Rose Seffanie took control from Aprille. *Now we talk about my cousin Micah.*

Haven lifted his coffee mug to his lips. He set it back down very carefully. His hand was shaking.

————————————

It had never bothered Dodo that her husband barely knew his cousins. She didn't know half her cousins, either, because they were scattered all over the country. Ev and Joan Nearing had been so difficult that visits to her in-laws were torture. As for Tommy Nearing and his father and mother, Dodo had met them, but basically the Ferris contingent were just names on a Christmas card list.

In all this time in Charlotte, we've never even driven down to Ferris, she thought. But that's reasonable, isn't it? Our lives are here.

She told herself that the Nearing cousins probably hadn't known each other that well. After all, Tommy had been graduated from high school several years before Haven. Age differences mattered when you were young. It was that simple.

But this MacBurton Ward thing, with its four unidentified would-be killers.

The possible killing of Miss Chrissy.

The missing Micah.

White men named Nearing who killed Black men for a hobby.

Rose Seffanie's narrative was not simple.

Dodo had an awful feeling that maybe nothing would be simple again.

Nineteen sixty-three.

Haven sank into a past so dark it was a circle of hell.

For ten days that May, in Birmingham, Alabama, the most seg-regated city in America, police used high-pressure water hoses and Alsatian dogs to disperse civil rights parades. Many of the marchers were children.

Before Birmingham, few whites in America considered segre-gation or desegregation particularly compelling. By the end of May, having seen elementary school children knocked off their feet by the force of the water, more than half of America said it was a huge issue and must be addressed immediately.

Haven's father had hated President Kennedy; how he shoved Governor Wallace of Alabama around. But Ev reserved his true hate for that self-righteous Martin Luther King, Jr., who pranced at the head of Birmingham subversive activities.

One of Ev's boys, who worked at the dealership, keeping cars on the lot spotless, had spoken up in favor of the president. Said his MeeMaw had John F. Kennedy's photograph on her wall, right next to the portrait of Martin Luther King, Jr.

It was inconceivable now that Ev had reacted with such fury, beating that boy so bad. The man never really got the use of his arm again, in part because hospitals were also segregated and treatment was hard to come by.

Rose Seffanie had to know about Ev's violence, but today she was concentrating on Tommy Senior, the man in whose house she cooked meals. She was using the media brilliantly. Haven remembered sitting in the kitchen, waiting for fresh biscuits to come out of the oven, listening to her read Bible chapters in a voice as liquid and flowing as the King James. Unlike Haven, she could pronounce anything in the Bible, all those crazy names like Melchizedek or Ahithophel. But for television, she had chosen the dialect of her childhood to tell the story of a boy whose adulthood never came. She wanted to waken every memory, every sense, of that terrible year. She wanted to find out where the bodies were buried. Specifically, the body of her cousin Micah.

Micah had been killed in a confrontation with Tommy Senior not long after Haven's father broke his employee's arm. Maybe Uncle Tommy felt he'd been one-upped and had to match his brother colored for colored.

The Nearings had been on their beautiful screened porch, with

lounge chairs and tables and potted plants. Uncle Tommy was having a beer. Actually, he was having many beers. He pretty much spent his life soused. He was supervising Micah, who was replacing some siding on a shed and didn't need supervision to do it.

Haven and Young Tommy were hunched over a table, studying a road map, planning a hunting weekend. Haven was barely eighteen and always felt honored when the twenty-five-year-old Tommy wanted his company.

Tommy's bride was out shopping.

Micah was a way better student than Haven or Young Tommy, although, of course, he went to the colored high school, so although he was roughly the same age as Haven, they'd never gone to school together. Micah was beside himself with delight about going to college. He'd break out of Ferris, get a real education, and one day earn enough money to help his whole family. He had danced around the shed and he hadn't timed it well. Tommy Senior was sitting right there on the porch, muttering into his beer. "I'm not payin' you to do vaudeville."

"Gon-na have a dee-gree," Micah sang, twirling his hammer, adding a drum roll with his feet.

Tommy Senior—who had no degree, whose family had never even thought about college, let alone gone—stomped down the steps and strode across the grass.

Haven looked up. Micah looked up.

Uncle Tommy snatched the hammer out of Micah's hand. "Don't you be uppity with me!" he shouted.

Uppity.

The great transgression.

Uncle Tommy swung the hammer once. That was all it took.

Haven heard the skull crack and the body thud in the dirt.

He heard bees buzzing in the flowers but it was his own head buzzing, his own shock.

Tommy Senior shrugged and walked back up onto the porch. "Bury it," he said to his son and his nephew.

Haven thought now, Why do I call it a confrontation? They didn't confront each other. Micah was murdered in cold blood. Very cold. My uncle and my father were reptiles.

Muffin stared at the solid, sober woman on television who had once been slender Stefanie. She was always surprised by women who allowed that much weight gain. In her heart of hearts, she thought less of them.

She had a sudden memory of a day when she and Stefanie were the only ones in the house. Stefanie had crept up to her, hunched like a beggar. There was nobody to overhear, but Stefanie whispered. "Miss Chrissy? Do you know where Micah is? Please help me. I can't ask Mr. Tommy."

It was uppity to talk like a white person; it implied she could learn. It was uppity that her diction was precise, because to any other Nearing, she would have said, "Cain't ax Mistuh Tommy."

"He's gone," whispered Stefanie. To anyone else in the family, she would have said, "He gone."

There had been something awful about Stefanie's desperation, her fine speech alongside her cowering posture.

Muffin couldn't remember what she had said, how it ended. But I knew everything was escalating, she thought now. I knew Tommy Senior and Ev were consumed by rage. I could have warned that boy. I could have said, "At least don't dance about it." I could have said, "They want to hurt somebody and you're getting on their last nerve. Go to Ohio now." I could have given him my grocery allowance and said, "Get on a bus. Today."

But it had never occurred to twenty-year-old Christaphine to get involved.

Over the decades to come, Muffin read armloads of historical novels and mysteries set in Europe during World War II. She would think how despicable those Germans were who cooperated in the atrocities of the Nazis. Now she thought, *I cooperated in the atrocities of segregation.*

In her living room, in front of her TV, Muffin straightened up. I didn't *do* anything, she reminded herself.

But that was the point. She didn't do anything.

Eighteen

Daniel sipped his first cup of coffee. He loved coffee and was really into flavors and frothing the milk. He was thinking of getting a quieter coffee grinder.

And then, on the screen in front of him, Rose Seffanie Fortress all but accused Tommy Nearing Senior of the murder of her cousin Micah in 1963.

Daniel had never heard of anybody named Micah.

But the following year, 1964, when Tommy's father ordered his son to get rid of the *Herald Tribune* reporter, Tommy had recruited Daniel, his friend Webb, and his young cousin Haven. Tommy was a leader, and back then, Daniel had been too weak to say no.

And now? he wondered. Am I still weak?

Bringing MacBurton Ward to that oak tree way out in the country had not been a scare tactic. It had been real. The one shitting

his pants had not been the reporter. It had been Daniel. He couldn't believe they actually were doing it. He couldn't believe *he* was doing it. His mouth had tasted of acid and his eyes blurred and he hid behind his sheet and thought, *This isn't me.*

But it was.

I am going to hang a man. How will it happen? What will I have to do? How can I get out of it? I don't want to do this. I don't want to be here.

But he would do it. He understood that. They all would do it together and they'd be each other's prisoners for life.

And then—Christaphine.

Her screams. Her crazed driving. How she leaned on the horn of that station wagon and didn't let up. He was so busy gaping at Christaphine that it didn't register that the reporter had dropped the noose they'd ordered him to hold, was leaping forward and literally diving into the back seat, his shoes sticking out as Christaphine put the pedal to the metal.

At last she took her hand off the horn and accelerated down some almost vanished road that probably led nowhere. She'd have to drive across fields, bump over ditches, mow down crops.

The reporter managed to shut the wildly flapping, heavy door and they were gone. A cyclone of dust marked their path.

Tommy was laughing. Slapping his knee. "I love southern women!" he cried. "Damn! My wife is something else!"

Daniel had been saved. He would not actually hang a man.

He got a summer job out of town that year and then went back to college in the fall. In 1965, this place nobody ever heard of called Viet Nam took over the news, and suddenly there was a war and Daniel enlisted. In Nam, he saw more dead bodies and acquired more future bad dreams than his hometown ever provided. His buddies, upon whom he relied for his very life, included Black men. He looked back at the world of his childhood with disbelief and shame.

In the chaos of his Nam memories, some of which he still battled, Daniel had all but forgotten the reporter who came to Ferris. But no one could forget Christaphine. And now she lived a quarter mile away from him and Virgie.

What was he going to do?

Daniel could not face the resurrection of the almost lynching.

During an ad, Dodo muted the television. "It's you, isn't it, Haven?"

There was a pause, far too long for Dodo's sinking heart. Her husband seemed desperately sad. She wanted to pat his hand and tell him everything was all right.

But that would not be true.

That young man Micah had been murdered. Buried in a dam, perhaps, like the Freedom Riders. The Carolinas had hundreds of earthen dams on old farms in old towns.

"Yes," her husband said softly. "Tommy and me. Daniel and Webb. But we weren't going to hurt him. That was never the plan.

He was a scrawny little guy, no real guts. He was counting on his newspaper credentials. We were sure that if we gave him a serious scare, he'd leave Ferris like a whipped dog."

Dodo had been referring to 1963 and the missing cousin Micah, but Haven was referring to 1964 and MacBurton Ward.

"It seemed so simple back then, Dodo. Kind of like fifties TV. *Rawhide* and *Gunsmoke* and *Wagon Train*. You were the good guys, they were the bad guys. You flicked your whip, you brandished your Colt 45, and they ran." Haven closed his eyes, to ward off memory or to protect himself from Dodo's stare.

"Who was the beautiful girl who saved the reporter?" she asked.

"Tommy's wife."

"She was Miss Chrissy?"

Haven nodded.

Dodo had a hundred questions. But the answers…did she want the answers?

You thought at this age that you were finished with heartache. You thought that you had found peace and wisdom and perspective. But they were fleeting. You could still be destroyed in a minute. "MacBurton Ward never came back, did he?" she said.

"No. A few others showed up, but Ferris was too small for them. They had their sights on bigger towns and bigger conflicts. MacBurton Ward hoped to make us front and center, but Ferris was nothing much and there was so much action elsewhere."

Dodo thought of the thousands of major and minor compromises

in her marriage, all worth it, because she still had a good marriage to a good man. She did not want an ugly past to surface. She wondered if their children or grandchildren were keeping up with this. Nearing was an unusual name and Rose Seffanie Fortress had unmistakably repeated it. Dodo was a little surprised that none of the family had texted to ask for details. "Do you think Mr. Ward can find out your four names?"

Haven shook his head. "He never saw our faces, or even our bodies. We could have been anybody. We could have been forty years old or sixty. So even if somebody in Ferris remembers that Tommy and Daniel and Webb hung out together, and now and then Tommy let his kid cousin, Haven, come along, there isn't a connection to MacBurton Ward."

"What did the four of you do after that?"

"Daniel volunteered for Vietnam. He couldn't wait to go into the Army. Webb I lost track of. I transferred to UT in Austin. Tommy took over the family business in Ferris. The only person who could guess or know who we were is Christaphine herself."

"Or Rose Seffanie."

"No. We never talked in front of the help. Not on that subject, anyway."

"Did you have help too?"

"Everybody did. But my mother, as you well remember, was a piece of work. Joan couldn't keep anybody working for her. And my daddy wasn't just rough around the edges. He was rough all the way

through. It's why we didn't visit, Dodo. I couldn't have our children turning out like Joan and Ev."

"What did Tommy tell people about Christaphine leaving so suddenly?"

"Easy. She'd walked in on him in bed with some other woman and said he'd never see her again. Everybody believed that because Tommy was pretty much always in bed with other women. He liked variety, and he figured what Christaphine didn't know wouldn't hurt her."

I don't want to know either, thought Dodo. I don't want to ask what the Nearing family knew and what they did. I should help Rose Seffanie grub out the sins from under the rocks. But then my beloved Haven is in trouble.

Oh, Lord, tell me what to do.

But it was Dodo's experience that in fact, you always knew what you ought to do.

The question was—would you do it?

Haven thought about glimpsing Christaphine last Sunday at Trinity Hill. Out of nowhere, there she was, sitting maybe thirty feet away. Several pews and a wide aisle between them. He knew her instantly and she knew him. Stunned, he'd looked back down at his hymnbook as if she were the evil eye. Tommy's first wife? In his church?

How long had she been coming to Trinity Hill, and he somehow

never spotted her? Maybe she usually attended an earlier service, slept late this Sunday, and ended up at the eleven o'clock he and Dodo attended.

His thoughts had tumbled and smacked into each other. A well-mannered man would find her after the service, say hello, introduce her to his wife, ask about her life since he last saw her.

But he had last seen her at a lynching.

What if she talked about it? What if she told Dodo? What if—

But when he stood up for the hymn and looked back across the pews, Christaphine wasn't there. Was she circling the sanctuary, working her way over to come say hello? They had liked each other. Except now she probably hated the whole Nearing clan. And why not? Taking MacBurton Ward had been a hateful deed.

Except that there was no deed. Nothing had happened. She had prevented it.

People who went to church were supposed to forgive. Could she have forgiven him?

More likely, he was mistaken and that had not been Christaphine. Some flicker of memory, some toss of the hair, had confused him.

Now he stared at Rose Seffanie on TV.

For the first time in all these years, it occurred to him that if Christaphine had known where to find her husband, his three buddies, and that Yankee reporter under that white oak tree in 1964... she could make a pretty good guess where the 1963 body had been buried. Because if a place worked once, it would work twice.

Haven had never been back to that abandoned farm and its deep, dark woods.

Now he reopened the Ferris website and tried to find the farm road on the map. Back then, back roads hadn't had names, just state numbers. But that old oak tree hadn't been on a road; they'd driven up an abandoned lane from a deserted farm. He found his old home place on the map and tried to follow main roads to the vicinity of that farm. But there were so many more roads now. It occurred to him that he could skip places named Olde Englande Court or Blackberry Trace and their ilk. Back in the day, roads were named for the people who lived there, so that Mead Curry Road meant the Meads owned the farm on the south end of the road and the Curry family had the country store at the north end.

He gave up trying to find the woods.

"And Rose Seffanie's cousin, Micah?" asked his wife. Dodo carefully made a break between Rose and Seffanie, not eliding the names. It sounded like some other person.

"In 1963, I was a freshman at NC State," said Haven, omitting the fact that he'd been on vacation at the time and had been present at the killing of Micah. Hadn't actually seen it because his eyes were on the list he and Tommy were drawing up for the hunting trip. He'd heard the murder, though. The crack of the skull. He had been upset at the time, but it was the way things were. But now, sitting in luxury, he was shocked more by his own failure to react than by Uncle Tommy's violence. I went along with all of it, he thought. I

never even questioned it. To his wife, he said, "Uncle Tommy thought Micah was being uppity and he got way too angry. They were always way too angry, my uncle and my father."

But it had been beyond anger: it had been evil.

"Pretty sure he ordered Young Tommy to get rid of the body," he added.

Pretty sure? I held the legs, Tommy held the shoulders. We both dug the hole. We both dropped it in. We both covered it up.

It.

A laughing young man with a bright, shiny future.

Evil had been done and he, Haven, had literally covered it up.

He doubted if Tommy Senior ever thought about Micah again, but Haven had thought about Micah at every burial he ever attended. Micah, wrapped in an old blanket, lying in a wet woods. No prayers. No family holding hands and weeping. No gravestone. Abandoned like trash by the son and the nephew of his killer.

After the TV ads, Rose Seffanie was given another thirty seconds. Her voice and inflection changed radically. With no prelude or introduction, she said, "Men in our family have Bible names. Micah was named for the prophet." She recited the King James Version with authority and affection. Slowly and intensely, as if from a pulpit. "Chapter Six. Verse Eight. *And what doth the Lord require of thee, but to do justly and to love mercy and to walk humbly with thy God?*"

It was a famous verse and Haven loved it.

"Somebody out there needs to do justly," said Rose Seffanie,

leaning forward, staring out at Haven. She set aside her country accent as if it had been a cover story as well as a throwback to the old days. *"Find Micah for us.* He's dead, because he would *never* not go to that college he was so excited about. And Mister Tommy Nearing? He was the last man to see my cousin Micah."

No, thought Haven. I was. I shoveled the dirt.

NINETEEN

Tuesday morning, Clemmie had no time for television. She drove to Dexter River High School and taught three ninety-minute classes of Latin. In previous years, classes had been around forty-five minutes. It took careful planning to arrange good use of the new long periods. To keep both the students and herself interested and alert, she changed topics and techniques often. Clemmie believed in rote learning, so there was much recitation of conjugations and declensions, considerable memorization of important lines.

Her one difficult student was difficult only because of constant absence; he wasn't able to keep up. But he was a good child. She emailed him whatever he missed in class and he made an effort, but he was unwell much of the time. Every week, his class composed a letter to him in Latin. Once, after a lot of coaching, they had called him on speakerphone and chatted in Latin. The conversation

consisted mostly of helpless giggling, but for a few minutes, Latin was no longer a dead language.

Clemmie thoroughly enjoyed teaching. Still. She was in her seventies. It was a long drive to Dexter River. She had to be on her toes, literally, because she was smaller than every student, and she refused to slouch or sit, lest she lose some of her strict control. She would shortly have to sign a contract for the next school year and it was a big decision. Church and Latin classes were the pivots around which her weeks circled. But she was tired, the benefits of block teaching eluded her, and summer vacation could not come soon enough.

By three thirty, she was home, longing to sift through a stack of appealing mysteries from the used paperback store and a pile of enticing bestsellers from the library. They would have to wait. She had a ream of quizzes to correct. She fixed her afternoon coffee, got out a little bag of Pepperidge Farm cookies, and sat in the living room to savor her snack before she began.

The blank television screen reminded her that Muffin had texted, telling her to record yet another MacBurton Ward interview so that the two of them could discuss it. Clemmie never recorded anything. She didn't even know how.

She could not warm to the man. But how brave he had been all those years ago, walking alone into an angry town filled with angry men who shared an angry purpose. Perhaps he had been too young and too alien to grasp the depth of rage he was stirring up. He surely had not understood that it could lead him to a noose swinging from a tree.

Clemmie had not read much about the Civil War until she moved to the Carolinas, so she had started with Shelby Foote and Michael Shaara, moved on to Jeff Shaara, tried some Bruce Catton, and started visiting battlefields. By now she felt, as did some historians, that the nineteen sixties had actually been the tail end of the eighteen sixties. The war you left open-ended would just have to be fought again.

But reading about the Civil War was painful. She was now in an England-between-the-world-wars phase, reading happily about failing aristocratic families and collapsing country estates where gardens and vicars and cream teas had center stage.

Clemmie checked her email. Muffin had included a link to this morning's television interview. Clemmie clicked on it and watched Rose Seffanie control the camera crew. Listened to her deep, throaty voice repeating the King James: *And what doth the Lord require of thee?*

"Somebody out there needs to do justly," said Rose Seffanie Fortress. "Find Micah for us. He's dead, because he would *never* not go to that college he was so excited about. And Mister Tommy Nearing, he was the last man to see my cousin Micah."

Rose Seffanie seemed implacable. Unstoppable.

But she isn't, thought Clemmie. She's stepping into a murder that was successfully hidden for a long time. Murderers have long memories and long needs.

Her phone gave the glittery little cry of a text arriving. Muffin: Tell Virgie not to use my name in her golf article.

She's a reasonable woman, Clemmie texted back. You tell her.

Although Virgie wasn't particularly reasonable, and furthermore, she'd been getting forgetful in that scary way they all dreaded. Last week, she told everybody at cards, she had put the ice cream container in the pantry instead of the freezer. One of her grandchildren said, laughing, "Grandma? Do you need it to melt? Or should we rethink this?"

Bonnie texted. Are you going for groceries this afternoon, Helen? May I come?

In the deluge of needy neighbors, Clemmie had forgotten Bonnie, with her painful broken ankle and the walker she hated and the doctors who refused to give her a magic pill to make it all go away.

Clemmie loved the grocery store. She loved piddling around in produce, slowly choosing vegetables. She liked wandering down the middle aisles, contemplating the new and amazing possibilities in packaged foods, and then, as if practicing some peculiar twenty-first century virtue, not buying them.

Bonnie would ruin it. She'd refuse to use the handicapped grocery cart, because it embarrassed her, and would instead limp around with her walker, unable to balance more than two things on the seat, filling Clemmie's cart with her groceries.

And now Gale of the failed cataract surgery texted. Bought new playing cards with great big numbers. Barbara Ann and Bonnie and I need a fourth for canasta. You free tonight?

Clemmie never did anything on teaching nights but prepare for the following day. She felt cornered. Too much to do, too many people to shore up. She texted her excuse to Gale, finished her cookie, started on the quizzes, and the doorbell rang.

She had an instant horrifying vision of an IRS agent on her doorstep.

Stop it. It's not an agent. They'll send a dozen letters before they send a person.

Although there weren't letters anymore. The excitement of the postman's arrival had dwindled to nothing. Advertisements for cruise ships formed the bulk of Clemmie's mail, as if some central cruise-ship organization knew she'd never been on one and was determined to break her down.

The bell rang again, long and hard.

Clemmie wanted somebody *else* to handle everything. Of course, if it were an IRS agent, they'd gladly handle everything, including her future in prison.

She edged forward until she had a partial view of the glass front door. Oh, for Pete's sake, it was Muffin. Clemmie opened the front door, planning to be firm, but Muffin shouldered her way inside and that was that.

Fine. Clemmie would stay at the door and not invite Muffin to sit. "I forgot to update you, Muffin. I worked at the funeral reception yesterday with a couple I'd never met."

"Helen, please, I don't care about any of that."

"The husband's name is Haven Nearing."

"What?" screamed Muffin, literally clutching her heart.

"I liked them," said Clemmie apologetically. She decided not to give out the wife's name. There were too many directions Muffin could go with a name like Dodo.

Muffin flung herself into a chair. "That's sickening, Helen! How could you befriend them? I told you he was a criminal and violent. You know what those boys did."

"Except they didn't, Muffin. You really did a great good deed. You saved them from evil, and you saved the reporter from a terrible death. I Googled. What happens in Ferris after 1964 is a relatively smooth integration. A lot of ugliness, a little violence, but mostly, only a few years down the road, they're like everybody else, dealing with it and doing okay. Not fine, but okay. It's over with, Muffin. You're not going to give MacBurton Ward information, and you don't have to worry about Haven giving him any."

Muffin dug into the Pepperidge Farm bag and took two of Clemmie's cookies. "How do you know the man you met was Haven Nearing?"

"He introduced himself."

"And was he the one who stopped at that accident on Sunday?"

"No. That was a much younger man. It felt odd at the time when that man wanted to walk me to my car, and I had my suspicions, but it turned out he had something to tell me and didn't want to be overheard. He said the girls were on drugs and

completely wasted, and I needed to be more careful of stopping for strangers."

"Drugs are everywhere," agreed Muffin. "I was helping at the Food Bank on Monday, and there in the parking lot was Susie Kennett's daughter. The one who's shacked up with the drug dealer. Actually, I think she's the dealer. She was selling whatever right there in the Food Bank parking lot! I called Susie to let her know. Now there's a woman with problems. She sounded utterly incapable of doing a thing, so then I called the police. I mean, what about our clients? They show up with their kids for canned goods and there's this woman hawking meth? Helen, do you mind if I fix myself a cup of coffee?"

"I do mind, Muffin. I have papers to correct."

Muffin glared at her. "It's beyond beyond that you liked the very man I told you is a vicious criminal."

"I'm a bit shocked myself. But, Muffin, on that awful day in 1964, no lynching happened. Either those four boys would have committed murder, in which case you saved them, or they wouldn't have committed murder, in which case you were just a person driving a reporter to a hotel. I think Rose Seffanie's quest is more important than MacBurton Ward's. The missing cousin. It's clear that around the Nearing family, 'missing' could mean 'killed.' Muffin, do you have any knowledge of what happened to Micah? It was your family. Your in-laws who last employed Micah."

"Stefanie and I didn't chat or look at snapshots of each other's

families on vacations, Muffin. Well, not that colored ever got vacations. But you know what I mean."

Clemmie couldn't abide Muffin's offhand references to the old days or her refusal to pronounce the name properly. "I have to prepare for tomorrow's classes, Muffin. I'll see you another day."

Muffin stomped out the front door, pouty as a four-year-old.

Clemmie forgot about Muffin. Ro'Seffanie had exposed herself to people she herself said had committed more than one murder. She seemed to have relegated that kind of nightmare to the nineteen sixties, but was that a safe assumption?

Ro'Seffanie had dismissed MacBurton Ward: *He nothin'. And nothin' happen.* She wanted the people who knew where Micah was buried.

Ro'Seffanie is not afraid of them, Clemmie realized. They need to be afraid of her.

TWENTY

Some miles east of Sun City, down a road not yet gentrified, was a decrepit old ranch house surrounded by decrepit old cars and trucks. The house was occupied by a large group of people related in complex ways. They had several vehicles, including a few they kept for parts, another that could possibly be restored to driving condition if anybody ever came up with cash, and a couple long ago rusted out and abandoned. Their driveway was long and cluttered, their grass rarely mown, their shrubs never trimmed. They not infrequently left keys in the ignition—they didn't own anything new enough for a fob—figuring that their own constant traffic in and out would deter thieves.

When one of their cars disappeared on Tuesday afternoon, nobody noticed. If a car or truck was gone from the carelessly parked assortment, then somebody was driving it. That's what they were for.

Muffin got her hair done. Going gray was out of the question. She needed constant touch-ups.

She thought of Helen, still pretty and almost wrinkle-free, which wasn't fair. But Helen's hair had thinned so severely that she had an assortment of wigs. How awful to stand in front of the mirror every morning and stare at the threads of gray decorating your skull and then have to choose a wig.

Muffin kept her eyes closed, the better to enjoy the pleasure of having her scalp massaged. She loved the scent of a salon. But she could think only of Stefanie.

Stefanie had deflected Ward's search for the beautiful young girl of years past. No longer could he quest after his supposed lynch party. Now it was all about how hard Stefanie's life had been, working for those Nearings, and how hard the life of all domestics had been, working for whites in Ferris.

She told herself to think of Stefanie by her actual name: Rose Seffanie. Impossible to pronounce without dropping an *s*. "Ro'Seffanie," she whispered and the stylist said, "You following that too? I'm totally in love with that woman. She's so tough and brave. And she made a success of her life, no matter how that horrible family stomped on her. I love how she's a deacon in her church. I can totally see her in the pulpit. I hear her sermons in my heart."

I'm the horrible family, thought Muffin. Did I stomp on her?

No, but I never helped her out. I never even thought of her as a person.

Which forced Muffin to acknowledge her second and more awful reason for not wanting to be identified as Christaphine Nearing. Everybody would label her a nasty white supremacist.

Was I? Muffin asked herself. *Am I?*

Daniel Smith was shocked by the caller ID on his wife's ringing cell phone: Muffin Morgan. Which was to say, Christaphine Nearing.

Virgie was outside picking flowers. She had beautifully filled their miniature yard with perennials and small blooming shrubs. She had two bird feeders, a birdbath with a tiny waterfall, and two hummingbird feeders. She was a happy woman, which Ro'Seffanie Fortress and Muffin Morgan could end.

All those decades ago, after the shock and drama of Christaphine and her Ford Country Squire vanishing with the reporter, the four boys had stood there in the dust and realized fearfully that they, too, had to report. Tommy Senior expected to be told about a hanging. How could the boys admit that Christaphine had whisked the guy to safety while they just stood there and gaped?

"Maybe we don't explain," Tommy said at last. "We just say we handled it."

"But the reporter's still alive," Webb pointed out. "He'll go on writing. He'll write about this. He'll use his byline."

Tommy had an idea. "We'll say we thought a good scare would work better, because we don't want the attention that a missing reporter would bring to Ferris. After all, look at what's going on with the missing Freedom Riders. The whole world is down there, picking away at it. We'll say we had a plan to save Ferris. We'll say Ward shit his pants, he was crying, his nose was running, he was begging and promising, and we were pretty sure that would be enough."

"Might work with your daddy," Haven said, "but it'll be a hard sell to mine."

There was a panicky silence. They were all afraid of Everett Nearing.

Webb said, "I'm not in this anymore. It's a sign, Tommy. It's like God spoke through Christaphine. The Lord said, *Don't. Just don't.* So I'm not." Webb turned his back on his friends, walked to his truck, and drove off alone.

Daniel couldn't remember now when they found out that Webb had driven straight to California to look for work and literally never came home. Within a few years, Webb had earned enough money to move his parents out there too. The whole family vanished from the Ferris map.

Amazingly, when the three remaining boys got back home and offered their version of events, skipping Christaphine and fabricating that they had dumped the filthy stinking reporter at a busy intersection, Tommy Senior complimented them on their foresight. "You're right," he said. "I want to kill all these Yankee agitators, but

you kill 'em, they multiply. They're cockroaches. Scare 'em, we'll see how it goes."

Now in Sun City, Daniel eyed Virgie's phone. Christaphine herself was calling. He decided it was safer to answer than to let the woman leave Virgie a message. "Hello?"

"Hi. This is Muffin Morgan. May I please speak to Virgie?"

She doesn't know who I am. Daniel carefully removed any trace of his native southern accent. "She's not here right now. May I take a message?"

"Umm. Well. She's writing a magazine article. Could you please tell her that I don't want my name in it? Skip me even if I did have a hole in one. No name. No mention."

"I will make that clear. Don't give it another thought."

"You're the best," she said. "Thanks. Bye."

I am so far from being the best, thought Daniel Smith.

It had begun to rain. The sky darkened. People scurried around the parking lots of the shopping strip that backed onto Sun City, hurrying in and out of the grocery, bank, hairdresser, pharmacy, nail salon, and pizza place.

The stolen car used the busy side entrance into Sun City. The entry gate looked as if it required a code, but if you drove slowly within a few inches of the arm, up it went. It was a fake gated community. On the other hand, there were cameras everywhere, which

served as another sort of gate. Old license plates from a derelict car had been taped over the actual plates of the stolen car. The driver wore both a billed cap and a hoodie, rendering the face invisible. Nobody was looking anyway because of the rain.

Every garage in Sun City was attached. Every driver was swallowed by a descending garage door. Every driver was blind to other cars doing the same.

The driver of the stolen car also had a stolen garage door opener. The car crept into the garage and the door lowered neatly behind it.

Muffin loved storms. You felt so cozy inside your little house while they raged outside; so safe.

But she was not safe and she knew it. She listened to Stefanie one more time.

Somebody out there needs to do justly. Find Micah for us. He's dead, because he would never not go to that college he was so excited about. And Mister Tommy Nearing? He was the last man to see my cousin Micah.

Muffin finally got it. Stefanie wanted the missing Christaphine to tell her where the body was buried.

I probably do know, thought Muffin. Or at least I have a really good guess. But I am not touching this. None of that was *my* life. It was *their* lives. I was just passing through. I did my good deed. I closed that book and I'm leaving it closed.

It was a scary metaphor. Old books could still circulate.

I should go on a cruise, thought Muffin. Visit Mary or Robert. Just get out of Dodge.

She watched the interview again, and this time she wondered if Stefanie had decided to be a target. Stefanie thinks she can get out of the way in time, thought Muffin. Thinks she's smarter than men who might try to stop her.

Micah had thought he was smarter.

And then he was just a dead boy with a cracked skull.

WEDNESDAY

WEDNESDAY

TWENTY-ONE

Clemmie was up ridiculously early on Wednesday morning. Anxiety for Rose Seffanie, fear of her own exposure, the nagging knowledge that Muffin had needed more from her—every friend she had needed more—had invaded her sleep.

She dressed for school. She loved fashion and accessories and had once loved high heels, but they were out of her life now. Falling was a bigger worry than boring shoes. She chose her black wig, the only one this year's students had seen, and she liked to pretend they didn't know it was a wig.

There was a lot of pretending in Clemmie's life.

It was still full dark when she drove out of Sun City. She rolled her window down to let the sweet scents of spring bloom drift in. The fragrance gave her a pang, a sense of precious time passing.

At the main exit from Sun City, the police car usually parked there for the night was gone. What an awful job that would be: just sitting, staring, waiting.

I can't let myself do that, she thought. I have to keep my life going. No fair sitting, staring, and waiting.

Haven Nearing was not sure he had slept at all. He slid out of bed so that he wouldn't disturb Dodo and sat on the sofa, trying to organize his thoughts.

He had to act now, before he wavered and faded out and was once more a coward.

He dressed quietly.

It was not yet dawn when Haven left Cobble Creek.

Daniel woke long before sunup. He had slept just enough to feel groggy and unsteady.

He paced, trying to keep his breathing even. He walked a few steps out into the fresh air and the dark, and pondered his decision.

It isn't a decision yet, he told himself. It isn't a decision until I've actually done it.

Clemmie turned east on Route 75, drove through the pretty village of Waxhaw and on into Union County. The sky began to pink along the bottom. Daybreak was her favorite miracle.

Several miles later, she entered the parking lot of Pecan Pancakes. The diner counters were packed. She chose a little table by a window where she could watch the sun rise as she had breakfast. Company, coffee, and pancakes. Perfect.

And what doth the Lord require of thee? asked the prophet.

Right now, the Lord requires me to teach well, thought Clemmie, pouring on the syrup. I can deal with my neighbors' problems later.

Or never. Never sounds good.

Especially with Muffin.

Muffin ran against traffic in the golf-cart lane. It was way too early for golf carts. Or cars, for that matter.

The first part of her run, she faced east, where the horizon was just turning pink.

She planned her day. She had some shopping to do, but she couldn't get her mind on it. MacBurton Ward was about to launch a search for Miss Chrissy. He'd get the police on board. Cops in Ferris now were two generations removed from the buddies of Tommy Senior and Ev, two generations removed from segregation altogether. They'd love a cold case, addressing ancient wrongs in their town.

Stefanie had to know Miss Chrissy's real name. She'd made a mystery of it on TV to get attention, but she'd tell the police, and the search wouldn't be in earthen dams. It would be on Facebook and marriage records and Ancestry.com. They'd find her.

Now the first rays of the rising sun leaped up out of soft ribbons of color. In the piercing bright light, she saw how silly she was, how melodramatic. Stefanie had glared into the camera, trumpeting her Bible verses. But it was fifty years ago and nobody cared, and that was the whole problem MacBurton Ward and Stefanie faced. They and their squawks for attention would also be history in a day or a week, when something truly interesting surfaced.

Tonight she had mah-jongg at Binney Williams's house. The eight of them were a tough crowd. Helen had subbed once and said, "Never again. I don't have a Fight Night personality."

Muffin picked up the pace.

Last month, when he had gotten nowhere in his search for the four men, MacBurton Ward had tried to get an interview with a Columbia, South Carolina, television station because Ferris was, after all, a South Carolina story. But the producer laughed at the idea of covering a crime that (A) didn't happen and (B) was practically antique. Ward had then called the Columbia newspaper and had reached a reporter on the phone, but the woman said, "You text me if you actually get anything, but at this point, I don't see a story for us."

So he had tried Charlotte, a city on the North/South Carolina border that might be intrigued. "Well, it is a very slow week," came the unenthusiastic response. "I guess we could fit in a very slow story."

But he was on, and from there had the great good luck of landing a few other slots. A newspaper article was picked up by a news service. When Ro'Seffanie Fortress appeared, she was such a dominant personality that Ward knew he was in the catbird seat.

But overnight, a university scandal, a celebrity divorce, terrorists abroad, a local pedophile, and a utility company billing scam blew up. Jubilant reporters were rushing around gathering real dirt, today's dirt.

He tried Columbia again. An assistant producer said politely, "We looked at your clips, Mr. Ward, but we don't think you have a story. It's amazing you got any coverage at all for a crime that didn't happen."

"But Mrs. Fortress made it sound as if people were murdered."

"She was very dramatic. But it was conjecture. Good afternoon."

"I have ongoing research," said Ward quickly, "and—"

He was talking to nobody. She had disconnected.

He was literally yesterday's news.

He needed something to happen.

Or maybe he could make something happen.

Now the sun was an emerging dome of glory in red and gold and Muffin was warmed up. Too warmed up. She began to work her arms out of the indigo jacket that was almost her signature. She was aware of a car approaching behind her, but it was on the other side of the street. She didn't look up.

It was lucky that Clemmie had gotten to school so early because there turned out to be an important teachers' meeting. As a half-time teacher, she generally skipped those, feeling that she had done enough faculty conferences for one lifetime.

"Well, look at this. Our Latin guru deigns to attend."

"Why, Miss Stephens. Do you know any of the other teachers? Shall I introduce you?"

Clemmie smiled and sat down. They were just jealous.

It turned out that the school board was thinking of cutting back teachers as part of a cost-saving effort. Required subjects couldn't be cut, nor popular activities like marching band. However, fine arts, foreign languages, advanced math, science tutorials—these could be trimmed. Latin, for example, had a part-time teacher and only a few dozen students.

Clemmie was not shocked. Latin had been dropped from the curricula of most high schools across the nation. She had been amazed to find this job at all.

There was spirited discussion about saving the tiny classes of

the most advanced math and science students. There was outrage against—or total support for—cutting printmaking, botany, and photography.

"Miss Stephens? Would you like to defend your subject?"

She stood up. "Thank you. Latin is the root of almost half our English vocabulary. Latin is the language of theology, law, logic, and government. Latin is the most efficient way to learn English grammar. Latin trains the mind. Latin is the language of Western civilization." She sat back down.

She knew from experience that none of this meant a thing to most of her fellow teachers or the school board. They would keep Latin or they wouldn't. She would teach in the fall, or she wouldn't.

She put it out of her mind and went to her classroom. Of course, it wasn't hers; Latin was shuffled around, stuck hither and yon, preempted by anything. Now and then her tiny classes met in a library cubby or even a hallway.

"Miss Stephens, it isn't true, is it?" asked a third-year student. "I'm really counting on fourth year. I need it for college."

"You need it for life," said Clemmie. "Ask your parents to write a letter. And then you write a letter. And now, let us sight-read the letter of Pliny the Younger, in which he witnesses the eruption of Vesuvius. It is not easy to translate, but it is fascinating."

––––––––––

MacBurton Ward received an email from the now elderly son of the long-ago brave librarian in Ferris. "This is a very small tip, Mr. Ward, but it might lead to the name you're looking for. I remember that my mother was counting on a new board member to help with the integration vote. I feel as if that person was one of the Nearings, and I think the year would have been around your year. Midsixties. But the board member moved away so they didn't have that vote after all. If you check minutes of the meetings, you'd probably find the name. Maybe that's your person."

Ward didn't have enough energy for another drive to Ferris just to scour ancient library board minutes. If they'd kept minutes at all, let alone saved them. Some local boards had scrapped minutes back then: they didn't want a record of how they spoke and voted. But it wasn't just media interest in his story that was fading. So was his bank account. He couldn't afford more nights in a motel or more meals on the road.

He texted Mrs. Fortress to see if she had had additional thoughts, and she texted back, Thank you, Mr. Ward, but I have personal situations to attend to now.

———

Haven sat alone in a booth in IHOP. It felt like the last meal before his execution, so he went for the sampler: eggs, bacon, ham, sausage, and hash browns on one plate, pancakes on another.

Then he couldn't eat.

Fear and doubt assailed him. Intense fear, as of prison.

What had he done?

Daniel parked the car.

The decision was made and the future was bleak.

There was nothing to do now except put one foot in front of the other, say meaningless things to Virgie, and pretend it would all work out.

The management of Sun City constantly issued communications. This included online flyers for the week's commercial presentations (audiologists, travel agents, carpet installers), the weekly list of events (dances, dinners, craft fairs, and softball games), and landscaping schedules.

But there was not news.

On Wednesday morning, every landline and cell phone of every resident rang with a recorded statement. The only previous occasion for such cross-community messaging had been to request people to stay away from a serious house fire and let the fire department handle it.

We are very saddened to tell you that a tragic accident has occurred. A jogger was hit by a car and killed. The police have cordoned off the area. Signage is in place for detours. It is not yet known whether the jogger was a Sun City resident. We will update you when we have more information.

TWENTY-TWO

In her second Latin class of the day, Miss Stephens was asked how the verb *legere* could possibly mean both "to pick out" and "to read."

"That's a good question," said Clemmie. "Romans thought of reading as the gathering up of words. You pick up a collection of words written on your *charta*, your leaf of papyrus, when you read. Now kindly tell us the four principal parts of *legere*."

"*Lego, legere, legi, lectum.*"

"Correct. And what English classroom word might we get from the past participle?"

Silence.

"What do you dislike most when I do it?"

That was easy. "Quizzes."

"This is true. But I want a word having to do with *lectum*."

"We're duds today, Miss Stephens," said her best student. "We can't think of anything."

"Lecture," said Clemmie. "I could spend every class lecturing you. But I don't."

Chip had no ride. He had to sit quietly at home and contemplate his dark future. He thought about the jogger, who had no future at all. Some poor man or woman who thought he/she was staying healthy by running ended up getting dead.

Those early-death types were the lucky ones, though. They got to bypass the years of becoming decrepit and mindless.

He couldn't phone one more neighbor one more time for one more ride.

He needed to call the office of the assisted living facility across the campus from Millie. He hated that word *facility*. It meant space, but it didn't mean home, where you and your wife had cherished each other. He could transfer furniture, photo albums, and favorite books to a room, or maybe two rooms, in such a place and then pretend it was home. But it wasn't. It was a facility.

He gathered his courage, tapped in the numbers, spoke to a receptionist and then to some other woman. She said brightly—excitedly even—as if people *wanted* to live in her facility, "Drive on up! We'll show you what's vacant!"

I hate the word *vacant*, too, thought Chip. Millie's mind is

vacant. Plus, how am I supposed to "drive on up"? The whole point is, I can't drive.

Bonnie was sick with anxiety. Muffin ran every morning. She wasn't answering her cell phone. Barbara Ann said that Muffin hadn't been in yoga, and Muffin never missed yoga.

Muffin? Run over by a car?

But Muffin did wear dark clothes. She favored black leggings. You couldn't even see her at the side of the road. *Please let it not be Muffin. Please let her not be dead.*

They knew so much about death, these thousands of retirees. They had buried their parents and many of them, a spouse. Some had buried a child. All had buried many friends. They lived with illness and pain and disease. They had pills and surgeries and skin cancer. They had DNR orders posted on the refrigerator and POAs with a son or daughter. Many had already paid for a cemetery plot and a funeral.

But death was still a shock.

And no matter how much they thought about death or witnessed it or mourned it, death remained a stranger. Unknown. Unknowable.

And now, very possibly, Muffin knew.

I never worried about Muffin, she thought. I just worried about me. *Oh, Lord, I'm sorry. I'm so self-centered.*

Bonnie stared at her pretty house. Muffin also had a very pretty

house. Well, they all did. That's what Sun City was—summer camp with pretty houses.

Muffin just went shopping, she told herself. She forgot to turn her phone on.

When school was dismissed for the day, every student in Clemmie's last class paused to give her a hug. "We know they're trying to drop Latin. We're going to write a petition, but there are so few of us. We just want you to know that we love your class."

"And we love you," said the girl with the most poise.

It's all right then, thought Clemmie. I can go out on this. I was loved. "Thank you," she said, hugging back, although she was not usually a hugger.

She drove home slowly, taking a circuitous scenic route, thinking about a lifetime of teaching. *And we love you.*

Love. It was all anybody wanted.

She passed a tiny country church, the kind you thought had disappeared. It too seemed to be loved—freshly painted, lawns mowed, shrubs trimmed. She thought about her own church this coming Sunday. About Rose Seffanie, sustained by her faith when the world had dealt her a bad hand; gutsy enough to deal herself a better one. About Muffin, who was unlikely to attend Trinity Hill a second time, what with Haven Nearing across the aisle.

Clemmie was completely exhausted by Muffin. She was not

going to church-hop with Muffin, helping her find the perfect church. There was no such thing. Clemmie was thinking of churches she had known and loved over the decades and almost drove straight into a cluster of police cars that blocked the back entrance to Sun City. She slammed on her brakes, just missing an electronic sign on wheels. CLOSED, it said. USE FRONT ENTRANCE ONLY.

Relieved that she had not collided with a patrol car, she drove all the way around. Three red lights and several minutes later, she reached her little villa, pressed her garage-door opener, and gratefully drove into the dark, silent garage. There was always such a feeling of safety when she got home, although she was never sure what had made her feel unsafe.

Inside, she took off her shoes, fixed herself a cup of decaf in the Keurig, and added half-and-half. She needed sustenance. From her Girl Scout cookie stash in the freezer, Clemmie pried out a Samoa, grateful that Muffin had not dug into these.

She sank down on her sofa, nibbled her rock-hard frozen cookie, sipped her coffee, and pulled out her cell phone, which she silenced on teaching days. An amazing number of texts waited for her attention.

Call me, said Gale. Bad news.

Clemmie was not interested in an update on Gale's cataracts.

Helen, call as soon as you're home from teaching, said Bonnie.

Perhaps the doctor had scheduled Bonnie's surgery. Or given her a boot to wear. Or opiates.

Phyllis. Her messages were generally schedule updates: who was hostess for what card game or Bible study.

Fran? Fran's only connection to Clemmie was Bible study.

Anxiety hit. Clemmie opened Fran's text. A jogger was hit and killed by a car on Sun City Blvd. I think it could have been Muffin. Has she called you? Is she all right?

So death was why the police had blocked the back entrance.

Surely not Muffin!

Except Muffin did jog before sunrise. She did run in the street. She did insist on wearing dark leotards and that L.L.Bean jacket—vivid blue in the sun but black in the dark.

People drove much faster when there was no traffic, which was certainly the case very early in the morning. The 25 mile-per-hour speed limit was ignored. Supposedly people went forty or even fifty, although Clemmie doubted those stories. But suppose they did. Suppose they didn't see the jogger.

Clemmie was already crying. *I wasn't patient. She exhausted me. I was actually hoping she wouldn't want to come to church with me again. I never wanted to hear her mispronounce Rose Seffanie again.*

Her landline rang and she hurried over. It was a recorded voice, but not a scam call. It was from the management company. "We do not have much more information about the jogger who was killed this morning on Sun City Boulevard. But we do know now that she was a resident here. The police are withholding her name until

they have notified her next of kin. Please keep that family in your thoughts and prayers."

Clemmie spilled her coffee on the shiny hardwood floor.

The doorbell rang.

She couldn't seem to think. Find a paper towel for the floor? Or see who's here?

She set the mug on the counter and unlocked the front door.

It was Bonnie, her eyes and nose red from weeping, tears still glistening on her cheeks. "It was Muffin, Helen. I couldn't reach her on her cell phone so I drove by her house. There are three police cars there. Two in the drive, one on the street. I stopped and asked the neighbors to make absolutely sure. It's terrible, Helen. The driver who hit her didn't stop."

Clemmie shuffled back into her living room and fell onto the sofa where, twice this week, Muffin had begged for understanding.

It was too late.

"Muffin's next-door neighbor is Kent Pearson," said Bonnie. "Do you know Kent? He doesn't socialize much. Anyway, he had a key to her place, of course, and he let the police in, and they found Muffin's address book right away and they've already called the son and daughter. Robert and Mary."

Muffin, like Clemmie, was of a generation that kept paper records, probably in a handy drawer near the landline, the paper calendar, and the chipped mug of pencils and pens.

The doorbell rang again. Clemmie had not locked it and Gale

walked right in. "I recognized your car parked out front, Bonnie," said Gale. "What do we know so far?"

Their voices buzzed. Clemmie was unable to follow the conversation. They could have been speaking Russian. Bonnie texted Barbara Ann to join them at Helen's, and she arrived in a minute, having herself texted Phyllis, Fran, Marge, and Virgie.

Clemmie understood the need to congregate, to share sorrow and fear. But why did it have to be her house? She didn't want to congregate. She wanted to be alone with her remorse. She found paper towels and mopped up the coffee spill before somebody slipped in it.

Fran showed up, but Phyllis was babysitting her grandsons, and Virgie didn't answer.

Right now, Muffin's children, Robert and Mary, would be arranging plane flights. Chastising themselves for not visiting their mother more; not calling her more.

Because you had never done enough.

They all dreaded a prolonged death. They all said, *Don't let it be years of dementia. Don't let it be some hideous, painful bone cancer. Let me get hit by a truck instead.* So Muffin got hit by a vehicle and died instantly, thought Clemmie. What we said we wanted. But we were wrong. We didn't want that. Muffin had so many good years still to come.

"The children she loved," said Fran sadly, "but almost never saw. They're going to come at last, and she's dead."

Barbara Ann asked for updates on everybody before she prayed

for the soul of Muffin Morgan, and into this dark and profound horror, Bonnie inserted the fact that her ankle was feeling better now that she had a real boot, Gale said she had finally filed suit against her ophthalmologist, Fran reported that Susie Kennett had skipped town and left no forwarding address so that her druggie daughter and the psycho boyfriend couldn't find her, and Marge added that Chip had finally called Assisted Living to get himself an apartment.

Oh, Muffin, thought Clemmie. Already you're getting only a fraction of our attention.

THURSDAY

TWENTY-THREE

Clemmie took a personal day. In all these years, she'd never done that, since her personal life *was* teaching. But in her grief for Muffin she could hardly manage to get dressed, never mind slog over country roads to parse Cicero.

Phyllis, who always seemed to know everything, sent a group email. Muffin's son, Robert, had arrived. He and his wife were staying at Muffin's house, and Phyllis had already stopped in to offer her condolences.

You never offered just one condolence. Most greetings were plural. Regards. Best wishes. Odd, thought Clemmie, that you "offered" condolences at all, as if they might be refused.

The daughter, Mary, and her husband had flown down from New York last night, Phyllis said, and were at a motel. Robert and Mary could not yet arrange the funeral because they did not have the body.

The day was overcast and slightly chilly. Clemmie decided to walk over to Muffin's house to greet the family because there would be so many cars and parking would be impossible.

She wore her favorite black pants, a shirt in a black and oatmeal pattern, and an oatmeal-colored jacket. Everybody commented on the hot, striking color of her indigo jacket, but nobody even noticed the oatmeal jacket, and when she wore it, nobody noticed her either. Oatmeal was the color of blending.

She tucked her silenced phone into one of the deep interior pockets, zipped her house key into the sleeve pocket, and dropped her tissue pack into a side pocket. She carried Muffin's Bible, which she had forgotten to return and Muffin had failed to claim. The leather satchel had a handle, and it looked like a peculiar rectangular purse or a miniature suitcase.

How happy Robert and Mary would be to have their mother's Bible, she thought. It's full of Muffin's annotations from a lifetime of sermons and classes and Sunday Schools. It's a treasure.

But when Clemmie arrived, Robert was paying little attention to callers. He was furious with Sun City, fulminating against the police, who had achieved nothing, disgusted that the cameras at the entrances had failed to identify any car damaged by hitting his mother. The callers smiled as they greeted him and he glared back.

When a neighbor winced after a violent handshake, Clemmie

realized that Robert really *was* refusing condolences. She slid into the house without even greeting Muffin's son. She'd give him the Bible when he had relaxed a bit. Somebody had laid out cheese trays, grocery store hors d'oeuvres platters, and a variety of boxed cookies and crackers. Nobody touched the food. Robert's hostility was so strong that even the least socially aware didn't want to be caught contentedly chewing.

Robert was a handsome man, even though he had to be well over fifty and carrying at least that many extra pounds. His attractive wife, though still slender, had held up less well, a testimony to too much sun.

"And on top of everything else," said Robert, his voice quivering with outrage, "they are claiming that my mother's name is not Muffin Revere Morgan! They are claiming she had another name entirely and a previous marriage! Well, she didn't! These people are—" He caught himself. Made a noun substitution. "Fools."

Clemmie was glad that Muffin's little Bible suitcase hid the inscription. Robert wouldn't want it after all. It was proof that his mother really had been Christaphine Angelique.

There was something familiar about Robert, and yet Clemmie saw no trace of Muffin in his features, and she'd never met him before. He'd never visited, preferring to pay his mother's airfare to come once a year to California.

Clemmie retreated to the back of the gathering, took out her cell phone, and Googled again the obituary of the first husband,

the young Tommy Nearing. The black-and-white photograph from the defunct Ferris newspaper showed a man roughly the same age Robert was now and almost identical to Robert.

Oh, Muffin, thought Clemmie. You never wanted Robert to know. But I don't think he can escape learning who he really is, who his real father was, who his violent ancestors were. Will the media learn it too? Will the connection to MacBurton Ward and Rose Seffanie and all those cruel Nearing men be made public? Will Tommy's other four children catch on?

She imagined those grown children and their spouses and off-spring suddenly arriving on this very doorstep to meet their previously unknown half brother.

Robert's reaction would not be warm and fuzzy.

How—and for that matter, why—had the police learned about Muffin's previous name and marriage? Shouldn't they be looking for more about the hit-and-run driver rather than more about the victim?

Clemmie didn't have the strength for Muffin's angry son and silent daughter-in-law. Either the daughter, Mary, was not here or she too practiced invisibility. Clemmie eased out of the house and walked home, texting Virgie, because there was one thing she could do: make sure that Virgie did not refer to the name Christaphine Angelique Revere. Virgie. Urgent. Stop at my house before you call at Muffin's.

Virgie arrived at Clemmie's the very moment that Clemmie did, so she must have been on her way already. Virgie parked very poorly, her car jutting out into the street. But it was an almost traffic-free cul-de-sac; people could steer around her.

Clemmie unlocked the front door and Virgie, the most kissy-huggy of Clemmie's friends, neither kissed nor hugged, but dragged herself into the house and dropped onto Clemmie's sofa without saying a word.

She really is in mourning, thought Clemmie, touched. "Muffin left her Bible here the other day," Clemmie said. "The one with her maiden name inscribed on it. I went over to her house, thinking I'd give it to her son and daughter because it would warm their hearts to have their mother's beloved old Bible. But Robert, the son, is very angry at the police." Just in time, she remembered that Muffin had confided the details of that first marriage and first child only to her, and not to Virgie. "Robert is distraught. I'll go over later and hope to speak to Mary and maybe she'll be receptive. Anyway, Virgie, this is not the time to tell Robert about the Bible or about the name on it."

Virgie began to cry. Before they could begin talking about Muffin's awful death, the doorbell rang again. Clemmie's house had become some sort of way station for local news, like the pony express. She was the inn where they could find a cookie and a couch.

She opened the door for Fran or Phyllis or Margie or whoever, but it was a stranger.

A tall, thin Black woman with a frown. Standing behind her was an immense white man with a sort of negative smile.

"I'm Detective Waters," said the woman, holding up an ID wallet. "Miz Stephens? May we come in?"

Detectives? At my house? thought Clemmie. Shouldn't detectives be out there measuring skid marks or something? Looking at videos from all the Sun City cameras? Researching license plates?

Unless they were detecting *her*. Maybe this had nothing to do with Muffin. Maybe it was something to do with stealing Helen.

Clemmie's mind went truly blank, as if she had just been launched on that slippery slide into dementia. She gestured them inside without speaking and they took seats without asking.

Virgie stared at them, crinkling her eyes and frowning as though her eyesight were impaired and squinting would bring these strangers into focus. Clemmie felt the same.

I didn't steal Helen, she told herself. I didn't steal anything. I just used her name. It's a semi-crime.

She needed to act normally. When you welcomed strangers into your house, you said and did certain things. What were they? Oh, yes. You offered them something to drink. "May I get you a glass of tea?" she asked, and this was such a solid, reliable maneuver that she remembered other similar questions. "Or coffee? Milk and sugar?"

"We're fine, thank you," said the woman. She introduced her companion and how they were both detectives, and already Clemmie couldn't remember either name. Virgie gave no sign of having heard

the names to start with. Clemmie felt a ridiculous and inappropriate giggle rising in her chest.

The woman said, "So we're told that you were good friends with Muffin Morgan, Miz Stephens."

They *were* here about Muffin. Well, of course they were. How self-centered to think everything was about her. "We live only a few blocks apart, so we see each other often," Clemmie said. "There are lots of neighborhood activities. And Muffin and Virgie and I are in the same Bible study." She nodded toward Virgie, who had taken over the tissue box. "Muffin and I were roommates on a bus trip to Maine," she added. She thought of the fall color of which Muffin had taken so many photographs, the shopping, the laughter, and the trying on of discounted L.L.Bean clothing.

"Ma'am?" said the woman. Her last name was River or Millpond or something. She was trying to get Virgie's attention.

"This is Virgie Smith. She doesn't live in this pod, but nearby. We're just—well—we're weeping together," said Clemmie.

"Mrs. Smith?" said the man detective. "I'm sorry for your loss. You also knew Mrs. Morgan well?"

Virgie sat up straight, folding her hands like a grade school child preparing an answer. "Yes. Except I didn't go to Maine. And don't we also play cards together, Helen?" She looked desperate, as if confirmation was crucial.

"Pinochle," agreed Clemmie. These days, Virgie had to be reminded how to bid.

"Do either of you ever jog with her?"

"Running, Muffin called it," said Clemmie. "Not jogging. Muffin was proud of running daily. She covered rather long distances."

"She goes out every morning," said Virgie, "unless there's a lightning storm or it's really, really cold."

"So it's predictable? You could expect her to follow the same route at the same hour?"

The question was odd, the way at that fender bender, when those two girls tipped their truck into the ditch, the man's question about *her* car had been odd. "I feel as if Muffin stuck to the two major roads," said Clemmie, "because they have golf-cart lanes and she likes asphalt better than concrete, so she runs in the golf-cart lane." Her verb tenses were mixed up; some past; some present.

Oh, Muffin! You are no longer present.

She bowed her head, covered her eyes, and in the darkness of her own palms, she understood that if detectives wanted to know whether Muffin followed a predictable route, they were thinking, or half thinking, or covering all the bases, that somebody had *intended* to hit Muffin.

Horror seized her.

Muffin had been physically afraid of Haven Nearing. She had literally *run* to hide in Clemmie's car. To hide from Haven!

Clemmie had chosen to stop for a meaningless minor accident instead of giving Muffin what she needed. In this very room, Muffin had said she was afraid of being killed. Had Clemmie been kind?

Proactive? Even mildly sympathetic? No. Clemmie just sat there during Muffin's endless narrative, thinking of the sleep she wasn't getting.

But if Muffin really thought Haven might try to kill her, she wouldn't have gone running at all, would she? She'd have stayed hidden, or done her running in the clubhouse on the teensy-weensy indoor track.

"Daniel," said Virgie suddenly. The word seemed loaded with meaning, with questions and anxiety. Virgie looked into Clemmie's eyes, and Clemmie knew that look; it was the same look Chip and Gale and Bonnie gave her. *You're the neighborhood visiting nurse. Fix this.* Virgie began crying without motion or sound, just leaking tears.

"You seem very upset, Mrs. Smith," said Detective Whatever-his-name-was.

"Of course she's upset," said Clemmie. "Our friend is dead." She kept her voice low, hoping to lessen the drama of Virgie's cries. Although Muffin had loved drama. Would probably love the idea of Virgie getting hysterical over her. "We all talk about death, you see," she said. "We pray that we will go fast. We want to keel over in a restaurant among friends, having a good time, except then the poor friends don't have a good time, but at least you're out of it quickly. We don't want to get pancreatic cancer or Lou Gehrig's disease or Alzheimer's."

Virgie's sobbing stopped. "Why did you say Alzheimer's?" she demanded, her voice going from slack to sharp, her eyes narrow and angry.

Clemmie was startled. "Or dementia. One of those nightmares."

Virgie's face crumpled. "Do you know what Daniel did?" she whispered to Clemmie, ignoring or forgetting the two detectives.

Why would Virgie bring up her husband now? Why even think of him in the context of Muffin and running?

Clemmie ceased to breathe. Virgie Smith's husband was Daniel. *Daniel Smith.* Could he possibly be *the* Daniel? It is a small world, she thought, but is it that small? Could two of the four players in that 1964 non-lynching live right here? Of course they could. Ferris was maybe a hundred miles south. Native sons might logically choose this retirement community. It was the first, and in Clemmie's assessment, the best in the area.

Muffin had said that any of those men might want to kill her, and since Tommy was no longer alive, she must have meant Haven, Daniel, or Webb. Could *Daniel* have killed Muffin?

Clemmie couldn't see it. The skeptical TV people were right. Nothing had actually happened in 1964. The boys who threatened and terrified MacBurton Ward were now in their seventies, if not their eighties. There was nothing to murder Muffin *for*. If Virgie's Daniel is *the* Daniel, she thought, the last thing he'd do is get up early, smash the former Christaphine to the pavement, and then park his bloody, dented car in his garage. He'd just wait. Ward's story is just going to evaporate when the news moves on.

On the other hand, who was better positioned to observe Muffin's running patterns? Muffin passed Virgie's cul-de-sac to

reach the main boulevard. If Virgie had told Daniel about the Bible inscription—which she surely had; she told everybody everything—then he knew Muffin's real name. He would have known even before Muffin told Clemmie.

"It's terrible," Virgie whispered. "Daniel did it. He talked about it, but I never thought he'd really do it."

Daniel did it? But how could Virgie be sure? Could she have examined the front end of Daniel's car and seen damage or blood?

Virgie wiped her tears with the back of her hand, like a toddler. "I hate him," she confided to Clemmie. She had definitely forgotten that police were listening to every word. "He did it, Helen. He really did it."

"But how do you know that, Virgie?"

"Well, I was *there*, of course. I was in the *car*."

In the car? Had Virgie been along to identify Muffin for Daniel? So that he killed the right jogger? Were they both killers? Did Clemmie need to stop Virgie from talking any further? Call a lawyer for Virgie? "You were in the car," she repeated, not wanting to believe it. Sometimes Virgie's sentences were muddled. Surely this was one of those times.

"Of course I was in the car," said Virgie. "But I didn't get to drive, he doesn't let me drive. He'll be mad that I drove here. But I had to talk to somebody."

The detectives exchanged looks. The man quietly withdrew and went out the front door. He was probably going to check the front

end of Virgie's car. He could see all of it just standing in the doorway, because Virgie had parked so badly.

"Daniel forced me to go," said Virgie.

Muffin was right, thought Clemmie. They were monsters, those young men. I was wrong. They didn't grow out of it.

"The morning of Muffin," said Virgie. "Which is neither here nor there. We had the first appointment. Daniel said he'd lose his nerve if he had to wait all day. He made me take all those tests for Alzheimer's. Those doctor tests, where you have to name presidents. And draw clock hands. I couldn't think of anybody and I got my hands backward, but it doesn't matter! None of that matters! I hate him. I hate him for saying I'm losing my mind. He won't let me drive, he won't let me use the stove, he won't let me do anything! I won't take that medicine. Which the doctor prescribed. Which Daniel picked up at CVS. I'm not going back to Daniel ever. I hate him. Our marriage is over. I'm calling our daughter. She'll come and get me."

Clemmie could not swallow the lump in her throat.

Virgie's only daughter had died years ago of breast cancer.

How they all protected each other. How the girlfriends stepped up.

They covered each other's mental and physical lapses. They went on playing cards and golfing and making useless pretty objects in pottery, and let the mental failures be. The failures, however, had become too many and too much for Daniel.

Clemmie wondered if Virgie's little articles for the magazine were actually written by Daniel.

"Car's fine," said the detective to his colleague.

"Of course it's fine!" snapped Virgie. "I am an excellent driver. I have never had a ticket ever for anything, not ever. So there. And he's going to keep the keys! I won't have a set. I'll be like Chip. I'll have to beg for rides. I hate him."

Clemmie prayed for Virgie and Daniel. Then she ran down the list of ailing neighbors, threw in poor old Susie Kennett, whom she felt as if she actually knew by now, and prayed for all of them too. She scrolled through contacts on her phone and called Virgie's landline. "Hello, Daniel. It's Helen Stephens. Virgie drove down here and told me about the doctor's diagnosis. We're not doing well. We need you."

"Oh, thank God! I fell asleep in front of the TV. I didn't realize she was gone until a minute ago. I didn't have a clue where she went. I should have taken her keys away. Just when it's really bad, Helen, it's worse. She's got the car. I'll come in the golf cart. Remind me what your house number is."

The woman detective was asking Virgie if she wanted coffee, and Virgie was saying yes, she liked hazelnut, and the woman was looking through the Keurig offerings on the kitchen counter and even finding hazelnut, which Clemmie couldn't remember ever buying. Virgie seemed to have forgotten her outburst. How kind and good the policewoman was. Way more than Clemmie had been to Muffin.

Virgie added her own milk and sugar and confided, "You know, we don't have a Keurig. We prefer to brew a whole pot."

"Me too," said the woman.

Waters! That was her name. Clemmie had a surge of relief. So she couldn't remember buying hazelnut, but at least she had gotten a name back. She wasn't yet playing in Virgie's ballpark.

The doorbell rang but Daniel walked right in. Very Sun City and, at this point, very tiring. She wasn't a public concourse.

Virgie burst into tears again and set her mug on the counter. Daniel crossed the room to put his arms around her. "Hey, sweetheart. I'm here. I love you. It's okay."

It was not okay. It would never be okay again.

Virgie swam through her confusion and tried to piece herself together. "I'm really tired, Daniel."

"Me too. Let's head home and watch a nice Hallmark movie together. You like those. They all end happily ever after." He turned his wife toward the door and only then noticed the strangers. He blinked uncertainly.

"We're from the Lancaster County Sheriff's Office," said the man, low-key and pleasant. "We were just talking about Muffin Morgan."

Daniel nodded. "That's a tragedy. The poor woman. I mean, you do that running every day to stay healthy, and here it kills her. I don't run. I guess you can tell," he said, glancing down at his generous belly. "I actually knew her, too, although I didn't realize it.

Back in the day, she married a buddy of mine. But her name was Christaphine Nearing then, their marriage didn't last, and I forgot about her. I've been trying to think if there's anybody in Ferris— that's the town where her ex-husband lived—I should notify about the car accident, but I can't think of anyone. Her ex died a long time ago." He turned to Virgie. "That's my girl. Here. Use this tissue. Now give me a kiss."

"It sounds as if you left the house very early Wednesday morning," said Detective Waters. "Can you tell us about it?"

Daniel was focused on Virgie. He nodded vaguely. "Two days a week, the doctor sees patients starting at 7:00 a.m. for people hoping not to miss any work. Of course, it isn't usually the patient who would miss work, it's the family member. Most of his patients are… well… Anyway…we had a 7:00 a.m. appointment because I just had to face this. Get the show on the road. We had to arrive by six thirty to fill out paperwork and insurance and all, so we left the house before six. Actually quarter of six, I think. I had a hard time making Virgie dress."

"You see anyone else?"

He considered this. "Maybe a dog-walker. But I had my mind on…uh…stuff." He took Virgie's cheeks in his two hands and bumped noses with her. "Let's go home, chickadee."

Twenty-Four

The police didn't leave.

Clemmie held herself very still. Perhaps they were here for her after all. It was a twofer. Stay alert, she told herself.

"Here's what we think happened," said Detective Waters. "Mrs. Morgan was running in the golf-cart path facing oncoming traffic. She'd have seen a vehicle coming toward her. If the vehicle veered into the golf-cart path, she'd move onto the grass and escape injury. Except that she wasn't hit by a car driving *toward* her on *her* side of the road. The car that killed her was going the other way. It crossed the median and hit her in the back. She was flung face-first onto the road. The car drove over her and kept going."

Clemmie let out a cry of horror. Muffin would have seen the pavement and the pebbles and the tar coming up to meet her. She

would have thrown her hands forward and worried about her beautiful nails. She would have felt her elegant features smash.

Could it have been some confused elderly Sun City resident— like Virgie, say? On medications or skipping them or not really awake yet? Turning down a two-way road they thought was one way? Hitting a shadow that turned out to be flesh and bone?

And then what?

The driver would be home now, wide awake, staring in shock at the damage to his or her car. The driver would have gotten the same brutal, explicit phone messages from the management that Clemmie had. Was he or she now pretending this would go away? That the car could stay in the garage forever and nobody would ever know?

"The car didn't brake," said Detective Waters. "It ran her down and then swung over to its proper lane. We can tell by the blood in the tire marks."

Clemmie hunched her shoulders to shelter her heart. The police waited, maybe wanting her to verify that she comprehended the hideous map they had drawn—that a car purposely crossed lanes and purposely struck Muffin.

MacBurton Ward had been stirring up the poison of the past. Had Muffin been right? Somebody was sufficiently desperate to make sure Christaphine never identified the lynch party that that person got in his car and killed her?

Who would it be?

Not Rose Seffanie.

Not MacBurton Ward himself.

Of the four boys, Tommy was dead. Daniel seemed to have been otherwise occupied.

Had Haven looked across the church aisle and over the pews only to learn that Christaphine Nearing was alive and well and living nearby? That she could give MacBurton Ward the names of his four nonkillers? That it would be wiser for him to crush her than let her talk?

What about Webb? Could he too have returned? Could he also be living within a reasonable radius? Could those remaining three men have conferred? Made a group decision? Decided that wiping out Christaphine was their only choice?

It was ludicrous.

No matter how often MacBurton Ward appeared on television, the central fact remained the same: nothing had happened.

Clemmie wanted Muffin's awful death to be an accident. "You just saw an example of mental decay with Virgie. Her husband doesn't allow her to drive, but nevertheless she sneaked away with the car when he was napping. People taking difficult medications or forgetting to take them or texting while they drive—that could add up to a hit-and-run. Or drugs. It could have been drugs." She felt as if Muffin had mentioned drugs just the other day. Drug sellers. Something.

"Could have," said Detective Whatever-his-name-was.

"It was probably an outsider," Clemmie told them, meaning a nonresident. Everybody liked to hold outsiders responsible for bad things.

"Cameras at the entrances record tag numbers," he told her. "Very few cars came in that morning and we've checked them. It was almost certainly a vehicle already here in Sun City. A resident could have done it, gone home, parked nose forward in their garage, and who's to know?"

In fact, an outside killer could have driven in last week, parked somewhere, killed Muffin, and then secretly parked again. But the few parking lots in Sun City were checked every evening by the police. There were no hidden lanes or alleys, no overgrown vacant lots, no shadowy corners. All garage doors were shut. Overnight street parking wasn't supposed to happen and would be noticed, especially if the car was dented and covered with blood. An outside killer had to have an inside garage.

They could leave the car in the garage indefinitely. Buy a new one and keep that in the driveway, which many did, their garages too full of too much stuff to squeeze in a vehicle. Years later, during some wicked rainstorm, of which the South had many, with nobody looking closely at front ends of cars, drive to some remote destination. Sell the car there.

Or had it been an inside killer and somebody in Sun City Muffin knew enough to kill her? That was also ludicrous. You could get seriously irked with somebody. But that could be solved by playing cards in another group, line dancing in a different row, getting off the committee, swimming in the other pool.

And even though her friends and acquaintances knew that

Muffin got up early and ran regularly in the street in dark clothes, no one would say, *That's* helpful. I can kill her *that* way.

Detective Waters said, "Did Muffin Morgan ever tell you she was afraid of anything or anyone?"

Muffin's conspiracy theory now had life. Or death.

Clemmie did not want to bring up MacBurton Ward and Rose Seffanie Fortress and 1964 and four young men of long ago. She knew what gossip—especially internet and media gossip—could do. Utter destruction would be visited upon Haven and his family, upon Daniel and Virgie, upon Webb and every living relative of Tommy Nearing. Upon Robert and Mary.

Many years ago, Clementine Lakefield had come together with two other people, allies of a sort, and together they had done a terrible thing. Or perhaps a good thing—she still didn't know.

She thought of those four young men standing under that oak tree, joined in evil—and saved from it. She wanted to believe that their hearts had also been saved, that they were thankful for Christaphine's great good deed. All their lives, they would know— *I'm not a murderer.*

Clemmie herself did not have that reassurance.

Her cell phone rang. Local area code. No name. Probably a girl-friend wanting to talk about Muffin. Clemmie wanted to answer but she didn't want to be rude. She looked back and forth from her phone to Detective Waters, who said, "Go ahead and answer it."

Clemmie clicked. "Hello?" she said.

It was a warm, low woman's voice she did not recognize. The woman spoke quickly and crisply. "An arrest warrant from the federal database has been issued in your name."

"*Oh!*" cried Clemmie, punching at the screen to get rid of the call, holding the phone away from herself as if it could bite.

"What's wrong?" asked Detective Waters.

"It's just some scam, but they call me a lot. It's frightening, and I don't know why it's frightening, but it is. Somebody says an arrest warrant has been issued in my name and an agent is waiting to talk to me." Clemmie could hold back the tears no longer. She wept for Muffin, for those long-ago murdered and missing boys in Ferris, for all young people who make stupid decisions and it comes back to haunt them, as indeed it should.

The two officers had had enough of the elderly crowd. They headed for the door, having forgotten their request for an enemy list. They said to block the scam caller's number and not to worry about it.

It did not occur to them that maybe there really *was* an arrest warrant issued for this particular old woman.

TWENTY-FIVE

Haven would have said that his marriage had no secrets, but of course that was incorrect. It was hard to face Dodo, knowing what he had already done and what he was going to do next. He lasted only a few hours before he broke down and told Dodo everything.

Then he called the son and daughter who lived in Charlotte. "We have a family emergency. I need you to be here tonight. I did something you need to know about because it is going to become public and you need to be braced for it. Do not bring the children."

Dodo covered her face with her hands. She wouldn't even look at her husband.

Would she stand by him? Would the children?

Did he deserve such a thing?

The detectives were halfway out Clemmie's front door. She was startled by the sight of a setting sun framing them in silhouette. The day had trundled on in its usual oblivious fashion.

How primeval was the shame of ratting someone out. You develop loyalties in a minute or a lifetime, she thought, and casting loyalty aside is sick and awful.

"Wait," she called after them. "Don't go yet."

The man turned his head but not his body. He was almost free of this suffocating, Alzheimery, old lady crap, and now she wanted them back.

"There is a man Muffin was afraid of."

––––––––––––

The living room in the house at Cobble Creek was silent with shock. Haven's two children and their spouses gaped at him in horror. He was able to see that they were middle-aged and not in great shape. Sagging more than he remembered, and sagging far more because he had just slammed them with evil. His life and probably theirs would be radically changed because of his actions. But he had made his choices and they had no choice. They were stuck with his.

He felt old, but to his mild surprise, he no longer felt afraid. The decision to confess had freed him. "I'm letting you know first because I can't predict where things will go from here. I spent a few hours with our pastor, telling him everything. He set things up, and he is going with me tomorrow afternoon."

"Dad," said his son, who looked as if he had just rethought his

entire gene pool, planned to divorce his father now, maybe change his last name, "you need to have a lawyer go with you." He did not suggest that *he* could go with his father.

"That's what Pastor Jay thinks, but I'm not going that route."

His daughter began to cry. "I can't believe this of you, Daddy."

"I can't believe it either, honey. But it's true."

————

Clemmie didn't eat supper. She was nauseous from turning Haven in. She went to bed early, reeling from the shocks of the day. Lying down was worse because nothing distracted her from what she'd said to the police. She imagined Dodo, crying, *"Helen told the police to ask my husband about a murder?"* How could Clemmie face Dodo again? How could she attend Trinity Hill again?

Well, of course, if it turned out that Haven *had* killed Muffin, they wouldn't be attending church anyway, because one of them would be in jail.

Just as Clemmie was dropping off, Phyllis telephoned. "It's going to be a memorial service, not a funeral," said Phyllis, "and it's tomorrow morning at eleven o'clock."

"Oh," said Clemmie, trying to wake up, find a paper and pencil, jot this down. "How did you find out?"

"Don't you read your email, Helen?"

"I get to it eventually," said Clemmie, for whom email loomed as a chore. "But would you please summarize for me, Phyllis?"

214

"The daughter, Mary, emailed everybody in Muffin's contact list. She and Robert don't know when the body will be released, so they've arranged a memorial service instead at Red Oak Funeral Home."

Muffin was now "the body." A package to be released. "Red Oak?" repeated Clemmie.

"It's out in the country, I think. Near Red Oak Presbyterian, and the minister from the Presby church will officiate." Phyllis reported this excitedly, as if for years she'd been hoping to hear a word or two from the minister at Red Oak. "I think Muffin went there a few Sundays," she said. "I'm not sure how recent that was, but apparently she mentioned it in letters. Can you believe that Muffin still wrote letters? On paper! Of course her children never answered. I don't think they bothered to read them. They're annoyed by the whole letter concept. They emailed back, but mainly they wanted her to text. Which means the most they really ever wanted to hear from her was a sentence. Or even half a sentence. Maybe just 'Okay.' Or even 'k.' Anyway, they called the pastor, and he was happy to do a service, although he said Muffin must have attended Red Oak before he was called there, and so he wants Robert and Mary to spend a few hours with him and tell him enough about Muffin for him to give a eulogy. He especially hopes that one of Muffin's friends will talk about her at the service."

Oh my. That's where this was going. Clemmie said quickly, "And what do you plan to say, Phyllis?"

"I'm not doing it. I hate talking in public. You volunteer, Helen. You're a teacher and you're used to an audience, and you knew Muffin so well."

"No. I would just cry."

"Personally," said Phyllis, to whom little was personal, all was designed for exposure, "personally, I think Robert and Mary are rushing things. They want to get back to their lives. They'll have the memorial service and fly out that very afternoon. I don't know how they're planning to handle the house and its contents. They probably looked around and said, 'What do we want with any of these old knickknacks?' Mary probably popped the good jewelry in her purse and called it a day."

Clemmie hoped not. She hoped that Muffin and all the pieces of her life were precious to her children. But if there was one thing you learned in a retirement community, it was that people's children did not always come through for them. Robert's wrath at his mother's unknown first marriage indicated that Robert didn't think his mother had come through for him either.

And he didn't even know yet that his father wasn't his father.

When Clemmie thought of her own son, who also had no idea who his father was and who must never find out, she always imagined Billy as cordial and warm, affectionate and good. But they had last met—or, rather, she had last sneaked a moment with him—when he was a toddler. Maybe his personality was like Robert's—angry, cold, resentful.

Maybe *she* was the secret she needed to keep forever. She should not return to the uptown Charlotte church where Billy and his wife went. Not sit in the balcony. Not gaze longingly at the son she would never meet. Unfriend Billy's children. Stop collecting information about his family. Stop—admit it—stalking him.

But the hope of Billy was why she had moved here.

All the card games and all the neighbors in Sun City would not compensate for the loss of that.

FRIDAY

Twenty-Six

Clemmie took another personal day. She dithered about what to wear to the memorial service.

In her younger days, funerals meant black, but people rarely paid attention to that now. They wouldn't choose hot pink or raggedy cutoffs, but other than that, they just got into something comfortable. It was a hot day, the first in a week. The moment the weather finally got hot, you wanted it to be chilly again. Clemmie decided on a pewter-gray flared skirt, which she often wore for church, with a pearl-gray top.

She had a new wig, a fluffy, silvery pixie cut, which she had worn only a few times. With that on, she looked exactly like half the female population of Sun City. But going gray was a big step, even fake hair gray. She needed all her poise. She went with the dark, heavy curls she wore for teaching.

Since public places were often air-conditioned to frigid levels, she added a white silky jacket, but it felt too dressy. The indigo jacket was too vivid for mourning, but Muffin had loved it when the two of them dressed the same. Clemmie wept for a moment, remembering how much Muffin had enjoyed shopping that afternoon at L.L.Bean. It had meant far more to her than quaint fishing villages in rocky coves.

Muffin had taken so many photographs on her cell phone, all lost to Clemmie. She herself had taken no pictures on their Maine trip or any other time. She never did.

I'll have only the jacket to remember Muffin by, she thought. She put it on, felt conspicuous, and wore it anyway.

She Googled Red Oak Funeral Home for directions. It lay at the junction of two very rural roads several miles southeast. It was nowhere, but when she expanded the map, she saw that it was actually only a mile from a town she'd never even heard of, presumably where they got their clientele, or whatever you called funeral home users.

She drove alone. If you carpooled, you couldn't leave early or late. You couldn't avoid the driver's errands on the way home or the small talk you didn't want.

She found herself at a quiet crossroad where there had once been a hamlet. It still had a fire department branch, a few nice old houses, and the remains of an ancient gas station, the adorable kind with the single pump and the overhang on the little shop.

Red Oak Presbyterian was very pretty: soft red brick with white porches on three sides, as if it were a southern mansion. The church-yards and parking lot were wrapped in white blossoming spirea and intensely yellow forsythia, with bursts of camellia and azalea just coming into bloom, crepe myrtle and ornamental pear, rafts of day-lilies and roses not yet in flower. She had never seen such high-maintenance landscaping at a church.

Why hadn't Muffin stayed at Red Oak Presbyterian? It could have been anything: the organist was second rate, the minister had theological opinions with which she did not agree, the service was too formal or too informal—but Clemmie suspected it was simply that nobody else from Sun City attended. Muffin wanted to be among friends.

I wasn't much of a friend to be among, she thought sadly.

Adjacent to the church land was an immense meadow where horses grazed. Then came the funeral home, also brick, with long, slender windows facing the pasture. It too had splendid landscaping going uphill and down. It looked more like a wedding venue.

There was no parking in front of the funeral home. Clemmie fol-lowed a long, looping gravel drive to the back of the building where a row of handicapped spaces lined the rear portico. Beyond these lay the main parking lot, also heavily landscaped and already full of cars. A second parking lot was up a slight rise, hidden by yet more trees, hedges, and blooming shrubs. She should have set out earlier because this lot also was full. A funeral home employee, identifiable by his

dark suit on this now very hot day, was waving people onto the cut grass of a field even higher up the hill. Clemmie didn't enjoy being told where to park. She was not a fine backer, in spite of the wonderful backup camera in her wonderful new car. At least they were parking single file. Departure would be easy. But since every other car would leave ahead of her, she'd wait a long time to get out. And now she had to walk over the hillocks and bumps of roughly mowed meadow to reach the gravel, which was also tricky—little stones skidding out from under her flat, slick soles.

I'm more concerned with parking than with my dead friend, she thought.

She finally reached the pavement and the rear portico where a large knot of Sun City friends had gathered. "Helen!" they cried, and everybody air-hugged and smiled, and several people said, "I'm glad you're wearing your twin jacket. Muffin loved when you two dressed alike."

They trooped into a large, featureless room with soft, shiny wallpaper and rows of folding chairs wearing white covers, like little spring dresses. A recording of old hymns played "Immortal, Invisible" and "The Old Rugged Cross." On the long side of the room was the row of high, narrow windows through which the congregation could see only trees and sky. Like her favorite E. E. Cummings poem: *I thank You God for most this amazing day. For the leaping greenly spirits of trees and a blue true dream of sky.*

Down in front she spotted Bonnie and Gale, but all those seats

were full. She was ushered into a center row. She tucked her clutch purse between her feet and settled in.

"Hello, Helen," said Haven Nearing.

She had been seated next to the man she had ratted out. A man who might actually have mowed Muffin down. And he had come to her funeral.

"Haven," she whispered as if in greeting, but actually in horror.

Dodo was seated on the other side of her husband. Her fingers were knotted. She leaned forward and gave Clemmie a small, tight smile.

They know I sicced the police on them. But they're here, so there wasn't enough evidence to arrest Haven yet. Or no evidence at all because somebody else did it. But who? And why?

She clung to the idea of a confused, overmedicated driver.

A woman Clemmie did not know followed her into the row and sat down. It took all Clemmie's self-control not to climb over the woman's knees and rush out. This is how Muffin felt last Sunday morning at Trinity Hill, she thought. And I wasn't even nice about it.

The ways in which she had let Muffin down enveloped her.

But there were also ways in which Muffin had let others down. Clemmie thought of Muffin's refusal to pronounce "Rose Seffanie," as if in some ugly, cruel way, she wanted Mrs. Fortress to stay forever a woman who didn't matter.

It was entirely possible that the Presbyterian minister presided

over a beautiful service and gave a lovely eulogy, but Clemmie never connected to a word or thought. She was sick at what she had done and what she had left undone.

At some point, she realized that the woman on her right was trying to muffle her weeping. The poor thing was using the same old tissue over and over. Clemmie dug out her little Kleenex pack and handed it over.

"Thank you, Helen," the woman whispered.

You met so many people in Sun City. If you played games at the clubhouse, or joined huge enthusiastic groups like the Ohio Club, or sang in the chorus, or handled props for the plays, or swam at the pool, you met dozens of people, eventually hundreds. Faces merged; names were lost.

"You don't remember me, do you? I'm Susie Kennett. We played Hand and Foot once. You were subbing for Maxine."

Clemmie didn't remember Maxine either. Presumably there was a sub list, Maxine had called, Clemmie had agreed, and Susie Kennett had been there. "Of course," she murmured politely. Her Bible study had been praying for this woman. In her anxiety, Clemmie couldn't pull back the reason. Surgery? Desperately sick grandchild?

Neither Robert nor Mary spoke about their mother, but that was not unusual; it was hard on a family to take sudden death in stride and then get up and address strangers. Instead, a woman from Sun City, unknown to Clemmie, described Muffin's Sun City life. It turned out that Muffin had been a founding member of the Food

Drive Club, sorting and toting cartons of canned goods to various food banks, month in and month out. She helped shelve books at the library, was treasurer of the Shag Dance Club, and had started the Foreign Film Club. Clemmie had not known any of this.

Dodo gave a choked little sob.

Clemmie thought, Haven knew Muffin half a century ago, but Dodo didn't know her at all. Is she crying for the loss of a good life? Or because she and Haven are about to lose their own good lives?

———————

"After the benediction," said the minister, and Clemmie realized that forty minutes had gone by, "the family asks you to stay for the reception. And now, the Lord bless you and keep you. The Lord make his face to shine upon you and give you peace. Amen."

He had shortened the famous benediction. That left Clemmie even sadder. Muffin's time had run out, even in her benediction. She prayed it herself.

Haven and Dodo eased out of the row, leaving Clemmie behind.

They didn't say *goodbye*, or *see you Sunday*. They just turned their backs on her, which she deserved.

Unless of course, Haven *had* murdered Muffin.

Susie Kennett handed back the remains of the tissue pack. "Thank you, Helen. I've just had the worst day of my life. I'm so ashamed, I couldn't even think about Muffin during her own memorial service. I could only think about myself."

How well Clemmie knew this predicament.

She and Susie Kennett followed the throng to the reception room. At least half the congregation went directly to their cars. Nobody knew Robert and Mary, and besides, many of these people had come simply to honor a neighbor or fellow club member, perhaps hardly known to them.

Clemmie had to stay. She had to greet Muffin's children. To skip out would be cowardly. She was one of the last to enter the reception room. It was air-conditioned to the max. She could have worn a parka.

Spread on tables was the identical food Clemmie, Haven, and Dodo had just presented. Same triangle sandwiches, cheese, crackers, and fruit. The tablecloths here were much nicer. Theirs required ironing, whereas Clemmie's church had thrown in the iron, as it were, years ago, and bought slick polyester.

And there next to the cookie table—cookies from boxes; Clemmie felt mildly proud of her church's homemade cookies—were Daniel and Virgie, talking to Haven and Dodo.

The two men still knew each other? How well? Were they startled and delighted to run into each other again? Or had they been partners in a hit-and-run?

She shrank from joining them, but Virgie smiled, waved her over, and proceeded to introduce her to Haven and Dodo. "Helen," Virgie said warmly, "is my best friend."

Clemmie was both touched and threatened by this statement.

Yet another wash of shame covered her. *I look like a nice person, I act like a nice person. But I'm not a nice person.*

"We know one another from church," said Dodo in a perfectly pleasant voice. "Isn't this a ghastly coincidence, Helen? Both my husband and Virginia's husband knew Muffin fifty years ago when she was Christaphine."

"I had no idea that this guy I hung out with back in the day had also retired around here," said Daniel. He clapped Haven on the back. "One of those small-world things. We weren't married when we knew each other, so we never met each other's wives until right now."

"Both beautiful ladies," said Haven gallantly.

Dodo said, "It turns out that Haven's cousin was briefly married to Muffin Morgan. Haven actually knew her."

"Yes," said Clemmie. "She told me."

Haven was surprised. "She talked about Tommy?"

Clemmie nodded. "During those television interviews with Mrs. Fortress." I used her name on purpose, she thought. Even at a memorial service, I'm a prying busybody.

Haven and Dodo exchanged looks. Clemmie thought she saw actual hatred in Dodo's glance, but she must have been wrong because Dodo took her husband's hand.

The men did not ask her more questions. They did not say, *So you know about MacBurton Ward? The almost lynching? The last good deed before Christaphine left town?*

But it hovered over them, that terrible past, while Virgie babbled and soft hymns played.

Clemmie couldn't stop herself. "You kept up with her all these years?"

Haven shook his head. "I had no idea she even lived around here until last Sunday. I saw her in church. I recognized her right away."

He did not seem to realize that Clemmie had been sitting in the same pew. Perhaps he had not been able to see her or, having seen Christaphine, couldn't look elsewhere.

"And then yesterday," said Dodo, "the police were suddenly at our house. We don't know how they made a connection between Haven and Muffin."

"I suppose they just asked around in Ferris," said Haven, "and found out about her first marriage and that Tommy was my cousin. Anyway, there they were on our doorstep. Asking about Muffin Morgan. I didn't know who that was."

Oh, thank you, dear Detective Waters. Thank you, No Name. Haven and Dodo don't hate me. Although they may hate me later. Because that's the thing with murders. There's always a later. There's even a later when you *don't* murder the person, like MacBurton Ward.

"'You might have known her as Christaphine Nearing,' the police said. 'She's dead,' they told me. 'A hit-and-run.' She was a good woman, you know," said Haven. "And here they think poor Christaphine was intentionally run over. I find that impossible to believe. They actually checked out both our cars to see if we'd done it."

"Which was shattering," said Dodo. "And exactly why they thought for one minute that Haven had a reason to do that, I can't imagine. They weren't forthcoming. We don't know why they came at all, let alone why they thought one of us would kill somebody."

"But our cars are fine, of course," said Haven. "And I even had an alibi for the time poor Christaphine was hit. I met my pastor at IHOP that morning. We met really early because I had kind of an emergency and that was the only time he could squeeze me in, so I've got waitresses and ministers and all to say where I was when it happened."

It definitely wasn't Haven. Thank God.

But if it wasn't Haven, and it wasn't Daniel, who was it?

"I wanted to come," said Haven, "maybe to represent the family. To—sort of—honor the past."

Clemmie wasn't aware that she had started crying again until Dodo patted her arm. "You and Muffin were close," she said.

"Yes. I'm upset. I think I'll always be upset. I don't want it to be true that anybody killed her. I want it to have been a tragic accident."

The receiving line moved quickly. Nobody had much to say, but Robert and Mary probably didn't really want conversations. They wanted confirmation that their mother had been cherished in their absence and then they wanted to leave.

Clemmie found herself with Phyllis and Fran. "Helen, you so totally will not believe what happened to Susie Kennett!" breathed Phyllis, her voice hot with gossip.

Clemmie couldn't stand it. This was Muffin's hour. Literally her last hour. Clemmie didn't want to hear about some other person, no matter how serious her woes. "I have to powder my nose," she said. The ladies' room was a time-honored escape and it always worked.

She fled. The ladies' room was immaculate, bottom half white subway tile, top half painted a pale, restful blue. It had several stalls, and at least one was occupied. Clemmie slipped into the last stall, slid the bolt, and stood there, leaning against the metal for support.

Could she just drive away without speaking to Robert and Mary at all?

Of course she could. Muffin didn't care.

Women came and went. Toilets flushed, faucets ran, hand dryers whooshed. Clemmie waited silently in the stall, staring at her watch. How long did she have to stay before the receiving line wrapped up? Of course, she'd forgotten what time she'd come in, so looking at her watch told her nothing.

She glanced at her cell phone, which she had silenced prior to the service. There were several text messages, including one from Chip. Earlier in the day, he'd asked for a ride to Muffin's service and then called again to say his back hurt too much for him to go anywhere, but thank you anyway. Now he had written, Assisted Living called. Suitable place is available. Want to check it out with me?

Oh, poor Chip! So desperate about what was going to happen to him next that he needed an escort to view his new quarters.

Surely by now Fran and Phyllis had left the reception, taking

their gossip with them. Clemmie went to the basin to wash her hands, although she hadn't actually gone, so hand washing was a reflexive act. In the mirror, she seemed intact, no visible sign of conflict.

The woman washing up next to her was Susie Kennett. They gave each other the flat, semi-smile, no-eye-contact greeting that women distribute in bathrooms. Susie Kennett washed her hands very thoroughly. Perhaps she was a surgeon and always washed like that. Or she was Lady Macbeth.

Clemmie pretended to fuss with her hair, although it was a wig and required no fussing. A girl could always apply more lipstick, though, so she dug slowly into her purse and slowly retrieved it.

"You're hiding because you hate receiving lines," said Susie Kennett. "I'm hiding because I did a horrible thing. Actually, decades of horrible."

How does this happen to me? Clemmie thought. I'm so much shorter than anybody, but they still think I'm a good shoulder to lean on. She's going to tell me her life story, and I will have to carry it around and perhaps visit her and even bring a casserole. "Well, enough dillydallying," said Clemmie brightly. "Let's go face the music!"

Susie burst into tears.

"Or not," said Clemmie, bringing out her tissues again. "Shall we just slip away? There's no law that says we have to speak to Robert and Mary."

"I could never speak to them," said Susie Kennett. "I killed their mother."

Twenty-Seven

Haven and Dodo progressed down the line. They had almost reached the two adult children of Christaphine Angelique Revere Nearing Morgan. An impressive name, thought Haven, and a cruel, awful death.

He didn't know what he was going to say. He wished he could let Robert and Mary know a great truth: that he owed Christaphine more than he owed anyone on earth.

His wife now knew about that day in 1964, the day on which nothing had happened after all. Christaphine's great good deed. But Haven had a bigger date to worry about.

He distracted himself by wondering why the spouses of Robert and Mary were not here. Were they busily dividing up the goodies in Muffin's home? Perhaps they had never bothered to come to South Carolina at all.

The line shifted and, with it, his sanity. Haven seemed to fall through the decades. He was standing on a verandah in Ferris looking at his cousin Tommy.

The mourners moved up. Haven didn't. His feet and eyes were frozen.

"How do you do, Robert?" said somebody. "Your wonderful mother and I worked together at the Food Bank."

Oh my God, thought Haven. *This man Robert Morgan is the son of Tommy. Christaphine must have been pregnant when she left Ferris. I absolutely know that Tommy didn't know.*

Haven was reeling. He didn't have the energy for this. He needed all his strength for the ordeal to come.

Daniel and Virgie reached the head of the line. If Daniel also saw Tommy standing there, he didn't remark on it. In a hearty voice, Daniel said, "I knew your beautiful mother when she lived in South Carolina many, many years ago." He extended his hand to shake.

Robert Morgan all but flung Daniel's hand away. "My mother never lived in South Carolina until she moved to Sun City," he snapped. "The police have confused her with somebody else."

"Oh," said Daniel, completely puzzled. He looked around, as if wondering whose funeral they were attending, anyway.

There probably *are* two funerals happening here, thought Haven. Maybe three. Daniel and I are at the funeral of a wild, crazy brave girl in her twenties who gave us an incomparable gift. Robert and

Mary are at the funeral of their mother. The Sun City contingent is at the funeral of a fun card player and Food Bank volunteer.

He whispered to Dodo, "I can't think of anything to say to them. Let's go home." She nodded. He took her arm and they eased away, past the cookies and out the door.

———————

Phyllis and Fran were getting into Fran's car. They had come nice and early and therefore had a good space in the main lot. It was largely empty by now but the next parking area, up on a hill, was emptying out, creating a steady line of exiting cars. Fran butted in because she was from Long Island and knew how to drive in traffic. "I didn't think the son was cordial, did you?"

"He kept referring to some situation nobody knew anything about," said Phyllis.

"I gather Muffin had a previous marriage. I mean, who didn't? We're all on our second or third marriage, right?"

"Speak for yourself. I'm on my first."

Fran said, "I lost track of Susie Kennett during the reception. I really wanted the details. Can you imagine arriving home for your friend's funeral and there's some strange car parked in your garage?"

"I think that happened to Susie all the time. That daughter of hers is always showing up and mooching or stealing. Susie always gave in. She would say she was going to take a hard line and she never did. She never even took a soft line. She caved. Even though

the car in her garage had to be her daughter's, because who else would have the garage door opener, she drove down the block, parked in the cul-de-sac, and called the police. She didn't even give her daughter a chance."

"Wait up, Phyllis," said Fran. "You've been telling Susie for ages she has to *stop* giving her daughter a chance. Now at last Susie calls the police and suddenly you're on the daughter's team instead?"

Bickering in a satisfying way, they peeled out of the driveway of the funeral home.

———————

Clemmie stood motionless in front of the white subway tile and the pale-blue paint.

Susie Kennett had driven the wrong way down the road and smashed the very friend who had been praying for her?

She really *was* Lady Macbeth? *What? Will these hands ne'er be clean?*

"Well, not really," said Susie Kennett. "I didn't drive the car. But I'm the reason."

Clemmie's mind flew back fifty years. I didn't pull the trigger, she thought. But I was the reason.

It had been dusk. All the objects and all the people had been literally and figuratively in shadow: the words, the weapons, the dying.

And here was Susie in the same horror.

Living in a retirement village (not that Sun City permitted the

use of that phrase; they were an "active adult" community, although it was Clemmie's observation that a high percentage of the residents were totally inactive) produced many coincidences. You were never the only one who had fallen into a particular abyss.

"Because I've indulged her all her life," Susie was saying. "I'm one of those parents who want to be best friends with their child, and we do everything wrong because we're trying to do everything right. Dara got into drugs so young and so completely. Over and over again I would pay for this and bail her out of that and send her to one rehab and then to another, and all through it, I loved her. She turned thirty and then forty and still did drugs, and I still loved her. I was always saying, *Leave Hunter!* That's her boyfriend, of course, the one she deals Ecstasy and meth and who knows what else with. *Leave Hunter's sociopath family*, I said to her. *Just leave!* And she would say, *But I love him.*

"Helen, it's so complex, so strange, this loving of bad people. So I didn't call the police the day Muffin called me up and told me what was going on at the Food Bank, that Dara was selling crystal meth right in the parking lot, so Muffin called them. Of course it's a mistake to call the police while the person is standing right there. And when the person is Dara. But they had Dara in custody that afternoon, so at least she'll get three squares and a bed, and it's probably cleaner than her own house, but now she hates me. And I still want to be her best friend."

Clemmie had definitely missed a crucial part of this narrative.

238

She'd been thinking more of her own past. Falling into memories was getting worse instead of better. She was always fearful that it might be the big fall, the dementia fall, where she slid down to the place where the past looms large, the present is inexplicable, and there's no climbing out to have a future.

"When Dara loves somebody, she always gives them another chance. I don't know why she loved them to start with. They're about as far from lovable as it gets. *Just leave*, I'd tell her."

Best advice ever, thought Clemmie. She gripped the large, long handle of the bathroom exit and pulled. Doors got heavier every year. If she got any more fragile, she'd have to travel with a door companion. "It was so nice to run into you," she said over her shoulder, as if Susie had not just confessed to being part of a hit-and-run.

Clemmie left the ladies' room and headed for the reception hall.

Like everyone who leaned on Clemmie's shoulder, Susie did not give up easily. She came right along, talking and tearful without pause. "And here, under the front seat was a ton of it. Dara and Hunter make it, you know. Crystal meth. When you're as wasted as that, you could make any decision. You could do any evil deed. And they did."

Clemmie stopped trying to make sense of the pronoun assortment. Poor Susie was incoherent with grief and regret and love.

In the reception hall, the staff were folding their tents, or in this case, their chair wrappers. There was no sign of Robert and Mary. Perhaps they were in some little room somewhere, writing a check.

Or on the way to the airport, having given their mother forty-eight hours and it was a wrap.

Muffin, I didn't even speak to your children, Clemmie thought sadly. I seem to be keeping your Bible. I didn't ask Susie Kennett to expand on her confession because I don't want to be Susie's best friend. It's enough to be Virgie's and Chip's best friend. I've let you down, Muffin. Again.

Clemmie took a cookie to go—she liked Oreos; she still twisted and split them—and when she turned around, Susie Kennett had left.

She walked out into heavy, humid air, laden with the rich scents of southern flowers. The long, cool spring had utterly ended. It was oppressively hot. Her car seemed miles away and all of it uphill. Clemmie crossed the now-empty main lot and trudged up the gravel toward the second parking lot. It was swaddled in shrubbery and bloom, as if not just death but also transportation needed to be hidden.

She wished she hadn't changed to her pretty little clutch purse, because she had to hold it instead of letting it swing from a strap. It was pitiful to be so old and creaky you couldn't even clutch your clutch purse and also eat a cookie while not losing your balance on the gravel.

She struggled to add up what Susie had said. Dara had killed Muffin? The police had her in custody? This was good because they provided meals? But if Dara was taken in custody the same day Muffin had called the police, Dara *hadn't* killed Muffin.

Clemmie peeled off her jacket and carried it, which meant burdens in each hand. As soon as she reached her car, she would toss the jacket in the back seat, never to be worn again, and toss the purse in the front seat, to be consigned this afternoon to the top shelf of her closet.

Only two cars remained in the second lot, so Clemmie had been successful in one thing: she had seriously dillydallied. She glanced at the closer of the two vehicles. Long, blond hair and sharp features poked out of each side window, like a mythical creature with multiple heads. But no! They were the girls from the fender bender. Jayleen and Jaymie.

"You ruined our lives!" Jayleen screamed.

Clemmie stopped short.

Jaymie flung open the passenger door and leaped out, shouting, "We'll kill you too!" Her eyes and mouth were stretched open like a bad pumpkin carving.

Kill me? Clemmie was stunned. Why would they kill me at all, let alone "too"? Run back down to the funeral home, she told herself. There are people there.

But it was gravel and it sloped and she would fall and this crazed girl would get to her before she reached safety.

She remembered the stranger in the dark SUV who had stopped to help. *Teenagers as high as this, who knows how they might act? Anything could have happened.*

And anything *was* happening. Out on the gravel Jaymie was

241

cheering. Behind the wheel, Jayleen was accelerating. Gravel spurted out from under the tires. "Try to get away," Jaymie shrieked. "Just try!"

Jayleen spun the car. Gravel shot everywhere. Darting out of its path came Susie Kennett. Fingers outstretched, arms spread, body dancing, Jaymie leaped forward to cut Susie off.

Susie swerved and feinted. She managed to avoid being crushed, but only because Jayleen was a bad driver. A decent driver could have crushed Susie on the first try.

They hadn't even seen Clemmie. It was Susie they wanted to kill.

Clemmie's mind failed her. She had too many facts, all of them useless.

Susie was trying to reach the only other car, presumably her own. If she could get in it or get behind it, she'd be okay. She needed a speck more time.

Clemmie pulled herself together. "Jaymie!" she shouted. "Jayleen! You stop this!" She waved her blue jacket like a flag to attract a bull. The purse tucked under her arm fell to the ground.

The girls stared at Clemmie, Jayleen's head poking from the car, Jaymie's head attached in a bobbly way to a thin, jittery body.

"We killed you," said Jayleen in a puzzled voice.

"They just buried you in there," said Jaymie. "It's why we're here. To applaud."

Susie Kennett had reached her car and was struggling with the

handle. Clemmie could see why it wouldn't open: Susie's purse, and therefore her key fob, lay many yards away where Susie had dropped it in her flight.

Susie realized that she wasn't going to get inside her car. Her new strategy was to circle behind it. "Oh, no, you don't!" yelled Jaymie. She waved her sister toward Susie, and Jayleen accelerated. This time Jayleen wasn't faking. She wasn't spitting gravel. She was going to pin Susie against the car.

Susie leaped aside and saved herself, but ended farther from the protection of the car. Jayleen smashed joyfully into the side of Susie's car and then backed up.

"You two girls behave yourselves," said Clemmie in her sternest Latin teacher voice.

"It's her all right," Jayleen said to her sister. "She called the police the first time by the road, and she called the police the second time at the Food Bank. I think we drove over somebody else."

Their laughter pealed across the parking lot.

"It's the blue jacket," said Jaymie, rolling her eyes. "We messed up."

Susie tried to dart behind her car again and Jayleen went for her again. Now Susie headed for the trees. Jaymie was far quicker and herded her back into the path of the car.

Clemmie's thoughts spun like the tires. They killed Muffin by mistake? It was jacket confusion?

They had meant to kill *her*? Because of the fender bender?

And here, under the front seat, Susie had said, *was a ton of drugs.*

243

Susie had meant the front seat of the little gray pickup. When that trooper came to the car accident, he must have seen it.

"Run, Helen!" screamed Susie. "They're on crack or something. They really will kill you. They killed Muffin. They parked the car they used in my garage. The police are out looking for them."

"Get the jacket one first!" yelled Jaymie.

Those girls are wasted, the man had said.

Yes. Muffin's death was a waste. It had nothing to do with 1964. Nothing to do with Haven or Daniel or Webb or Tommy. Nothing to do with Rose Seffanie or MacBurton Ward. It had nothing to do with courage or a young woman's great gift to four stupid young men.

Muffin's death was because she wore a blue jacket and because twice, women in blue jackets had called the police.

The car slewed around, missing the crepe myrtle and forsythia, heading for Clemmie.

It was like some insane demolition derby, a clunker attacking two elderly women stumbling around in their Sunday best.

Clemmie rarely felt rage. Suddenly she was bloated with it. "I thought Muffin died because of something important!" she screamed. "I thought there was history and a noble deed and sacrifice. But it was just *stupid*. You killed her because you are *stupid*!"

Clemmie threw herself on top of Jaymie, disregarding the probability of her own broken bones. They both fell hard on the gravel. Clemmie hung on to Jaymie by the hair, that long shank of dry,

yellow straw. Jaymie's fingernails were claws. She tore at Clemmie but Jaymie was physically wasted as well as mentally. Clemmie, incredibly, was stronger. Maybe from fury that Muffin had died because of drugs.

Jayleen got out of the car and ran over to join the fray.

But Susie Kennett was wearing high heels—real heels, with height and substance. She took one off and slammed Jayleen in the back of the head with the shaft of the heel. Jayleen staggered and fell, and a moment later they were all four in a heap.

"Ouch. The gravel hurts," said Jayleen, who was offended rather than dead.

Susie ripped the cell phone from the back pocket of Jayleen's skimpy, torn cutoffs and called 911.

———————

What with the fire department just up the road, and two of their volunteers employed at the funeral home down the hill, help arrived in no time.

Neither Susie nor Clemmie could get up.

"Are you hurt?" asked the first man on the scene.

"No," said Susie. "We're old."

———————

Clemmie sat in a small parlor in the funeral home. She and Detective Waters were each having a Coke.

All the regrets of a lifetime were as nothing compared to her regret now. She had interfered. She had picked the wrong good deed, stopping for that fender bender. The result was an innocent woman's death. Hadn't Muffin begged her not to stop? Hadn't Clemmie said irritably, *You're fine, Muffin, just crouch down?*

"We've dealt with Mrs. Kennett any number of times," said the detective. "She's spent her life coping with her daughter. Dara has spent *her* life with drugs and drug dealers. Mrs. Kennett finally stood up to Dara and refused to give her money. Dara's reaction was so scary that Mrs. Kennett drove away to hide. But at the same time, she didn't want Dara to worry about her absence—as if Dara ever worried about anybody except herself—so she actually told Dara that she'd be gone. So before dawn the following day, Dara goes to her mother's house to see what she can steal. Food, televisions, whatever. Dara has her boyfriend's teenage daughters with her. Jayleen and Jaymie raid the shoes and handbags, looking for money and jewelry. On their way out of Sun City, they pass Muffin jogging in her blue jacket. A lot like the one you're holding in your hand, actually. Must be a fad."

Clemmie choked back a sob.

"So meanwhile, Jayleen and Jaymie have had a car accident in their father's truck that they're not supposed to drive in the first place. They don't have drivers' licenses. The officer finds drugs stashed in the pickup. He takes the girls to Hunter's sister's house. We can arrest Hunter if we can find him. But we don't find him. So

THE WRONG GOOD DEED

then Muffin volunteers at the Food Bank and sees Dara dealing in the parking lot. Muffin calls Susie, but Susie has left town and is pretending the problem of Dara doesn't exist. Muffin calls 911. She doesn't do this quietly or in a corner or from her car. She does it while she's standing next to Dara. What was Muffin thinking? She knew that Dara is so dangerous that her own mother fled in fear. But people never think that *they* are in danger. They always think *they* are in control.

"So now we're looking for both Dara and Hunter, but we don't find either of them. The girls and Dara make a second middle-of-the-night trip to Susie Kennett's house to steal anything that's left. No problem, they've got the garage-door opener. They want the microwave but it's built in, so they can't steal it. They just wreck it. They strip the place. On the way home, don't they pass the same jogger they passed the day before. Dara says, 'That's the one! That's that volunteer at the Food Bank who called the cops on me.'

"Later that day, we catch up to Dara and Hunter, but we don't find the girls. Hunter claims they're still with his sister, but they're not. So now we're looking for his daughters too.

"But Jaymie and Jayleen have decided to get revenge on the jogger who called the police and got their father and his girlfriend Dara arrested. Easy peasy. Muffin follows a route; they follow the route." The detective sighed. "It's sad. Muffin Morgan thought she was doing a good deed, turning Dara in, and she was. She died that horrible death because she did the right thing. But she did it wrong."

Jaymie and Jayleen naturally assumed there was only one person in an indigo-blue jacket, thought Clemmie. It didn't occur to them that there were two of us. I assumed that saving MacBurton Ward from a lynching was Muffin's wrong good deed. But turning in a drug dealer was the actual wrong good deed.

And mine was also the wrong good deed. In a way, the *same* wrong good deed. I stopped by the side of the road for Jaymie and Jayleen.

But you *had* to do the right thing! It was the pivot of life: deciding on the right thing.

"The girls know about the cameras at the Sun City entrances," said the detective. "They steal a car from their neighbors, people who have stuff of their own going on, we see a lot of them too. They park the stolen car in Susie Kennett's garage. After they run Muffin Morgan down, they put it back. They probably figure they have tons of time to drive it away later or maybe they figure we'll hold Mrs. Kennett responsible or maybe they forget. Anyway, they just walk out of Sun City and a friend picks them up.

"So now Mrs. Kennett, who's still out of town, gets texts from all her friends about Muffin's death. She comes home for the memorial service, and in her garage is a car she doesn't recognize. It isn't Dara's. It isn't Hunter's. She's scared to go in her house, and she calls us. It's the hit-and-run car. We know Dara and Hunter didn't do it. We have them in custody. So who did drive that car? Maybe Hunter's kids, the likeliest people to have a garage-door opener for Mrs. Kennett's house. We can't find them."

"But it turns out they're proud of their successful hit-and-run. They attend the memorial service to gloat. They take their father's car because we impounded only his pickup. They drive over—and sitting in the parking lot is Susie Kennett's car. Super-duper. They can get her too. Susie is scared, she runs like a rabbit, and they love that. They're nothing but predators, you know."

———————————

Susie Kennett's car had to be towed because Jayleen had damaged it so badly.

Clemmie's car was fine, but she was too upset to drive. A volunteer fireman drove them both home in Clemmie's car, while another car followed to bring him back to Red Oak.

Clemmie sat in front, holding her silenced phone. Chip had texted yet again, hoping she'd go with him this evening to Assisted Living.

From Susie in the back seat came a text. Thank you. You're very brave.

Clemmie texted back. So are you.

I'm responsible.

No. The girls are. Dara is. Hunter is.

You're kind. If I had acted years ago, none of it would have happened.

Taking action. Not taking action.

It was no easy thing to figure out. Clemmie thought of Rose Seffanie's quote. *And what doth the Lord require of thee but...to love*

mercy? Poor Susie had been endlessly merciful to her daughter, and look at the awful result. But that was not the whole verse. It was the middle of the verse. The first requirement was *to do justly*. Had Susie acted justly when she faced her daughter's deeds? Who knew? Certainly not Clemmie.

It was so hard to make clean, correct choices. Susie had done the best she could, and it turned out to be wrong all the way through.

But among all the good deeds that had turned out not to be, there was still one truly good deed to admire. Christaphine *had* saved one man from being hung and four men from murdering him. Nineteen sixty-four didn't matter in Muffin's own tragic pointless death. But it mattered.

Everyone who had been brave and noble in those days mattered.

On the one hand, I'm just a busybody, thought Clemmie. On the other hand, I can drive and I have a shoulder to cry on.

She texted Chip. I'm coming.

Twenty-Eight

The discussion was over. The questions had been answered. But somehow they weren't getting up and going to their cars and heading the hundred odd miles south to Ferris. They seemed locked into the shabby old chairs of the church parlor, staring down at the dull surface of the old table around which they sat.

Haven's kids were right. He should have had a lawyer here. He shouldn't have talked to Ro'Seffanie at all.

But he had, and now she knew everything he did about the death and burial of her cousin Micah in 1963. It lay so heavily on them that they couldn't even make it out of the church parlor, let alone to Ferris.

Haven was sweating, but cold and shaky. He was fighting tears, which he never did. It made him feel old and frail.

There was no offering he could make to Rose Seffanie Fortress

except the terrible truth. Money, scholarships, fruit baskets—they had no value next to the life of Micah. Maybe later he'd test those waters, but for now, his one gift had to be the answer for which she had gone on television.

He dreaded going to Ferris. Which outcome would be worse? Finding Micah's bones or finding a highway built over them?

And then what?

Would there be charges? Would he end up in prison? Would that be the close to a life he had tried so hard to live well? The life Christaphine had saved for him? And Dodo, what price would she pay?

Silence reigned. Haven did not have one more syllable in him. He wanted to evaporate.

Finally Ro'Seffanie said briskly, "We need to pray before we go. Haven, you pray."

What?

He had to pray?

What was he supposed to say to God in these circumstances? And why was *he* assigned the prayer? They had two pastors here. That was their job. His own pastor, good old Jay, had hardly said a word. Just flinched now and then. Ro'Seffanie's pastor—a former major league shortstop; a guy with a congregation overflowing into the streets, there were so many people who liked his preaching—he hadn't said anything either.

Ro'Seffanie raised her eyebrows at Haven, waiting. He sat there.

She jutted her face forward, directing him to begin. Then she folded her hands on the edge of the table, bowed her head, and closed her eyes.

Haven couldn't think of a single thing to pray about. There was certainly nothing for which he could give thanks. He had had a life with absolutely everything. And now, as his children had said, he was throwing it away. It was not necessary for him to confess, they cried. How dare he do this to them?

All you did was bury a body! his son had shouted. *And you were just a kid yourself! Leave it there! Leave this alone!*

But Rose Seffanie Fortress had needed to know and Haven had needed to tell. He needed to be able recite Micah 6:8 and know that at the last, he had acted justly.

His son and daughter and their spouses had stalked out of the Cobble Creek house last night, ashamed of him, afraid of repercussions. He had lost his children. Possibly his marriage.

Neither pastor rescued him.

Okay, he had to do this. It was part of his punishment. Haven managed to take a breath. "Dear Lord," he said. Although the Lord was not dear right now. The Lord was entirely out of reach. "Lord, please let Rose Seffanie find what she needs to find." He was almost panting. He had to pause to recover. The prayer needed another sentence. What could it be?

"Please give me," he began—but there was nowhere to go with that. Give him what? He had everything. Fine family, fine income,

fine home. But behind him, way behind, literally buried, was the terrible act in which he had colluded. Haven swallowed. "Give me what I deserve, Lord. Amen."

He couldn't look up. He couldn't meet their eyes and see what they thought he deserved.

Ro'Seffanie said irritably, "Well, that's the sorriest prayer I heard in years."

He looked at her after all.

She rolled her eyes. "You've been going to church how long? And you missed the whole point?" She leaned forward. "The Lord's not going to give you what you deserve. He's not going to give any of us what we deserve." Ro'Seffanie stood up and retrieved her handbag and her hat. "He's going to forgive us, Haven."

She didn't say she had forgiven him. He didn't see how she ever could. Certainly he could not forgive himself.

She thanked the ministers for coming. "You drive," she ordered Haven. "We'll be fine, Haven and me," she said to Pastor Jay, who looked nervous. "He knew Ferris from the top down and I knew Ferris from the bottom up. We have a lot to talk about. We won't solve the problems of the world, but at least we can sit side by side."

They climbed into Haven's car. He was relieved to see that he had a full tank of gas. He headed for the highway. He turned south. After a while, he said, "What if we find the right woods?"

"We won't," she said softly. "You know that. Nothing's the same. Those roads didn't even have names then, and those woods? Cut

down years ago. Subdivisions, probably. Condos. Apartments. Strip malls. I just want to get out of the car, somewhere near, and say a prayer for Micah. Maybe cry a little. Maybe drive through Ferris. No matter whether the old houses are standing, that old life was cut down years ago too. You and me, Haven, we're the history of our town. Long ago and far away, thank the Lord."

Ro'Seffanie leaned forward, tuned the radio to a gospel station, and turned up the volume.

READING GROUP GUIDE

1. What does it cost Clemmie to stay silent about her past? Is there any potential alternative?

2. The news exhausts Clemmie, especially because she doesn't feel like she can affect it. Now that you can access the news from anywhere, at any time, how can you prevent it from overwhelming you? How does the pace of the news bury stories that don't have satisfying endings?

3. After saving MacBurton Ward, Muffin realizes she can never return home. Would you have made the same choice if you knew it meant you'd have to start over somewhere else?

4. Clemmie recalls that during the trials of integration, she was "that questionable thing: the bystander." Do you think our expectations of bystanders have changed since 1964? How?

5. Muffin decides to stay silent about Micah's death partially out of respect to her ex-husband's living children. Should you protect anyone's reputation if it prevents justice?

6. Daniel assures himself that he is innocent because Muffin intervened before any crimes had been committed. Is he right?

7. Clemmie frequently thinks of herself as a bad person despite her best attempts to live a good life. Do you think people can redeem themselves even if their guilt never passes?

8. What did you think of Muffin's inability or unwillingness to change how she referred to Ro'Seffanie when she learned her real name? How else does her stubbornness appear throughout the book?

9. Discuss Haven Nearing. What kind of closure did he give to Ro'Seffanie, and what kind of closure does he himself need?

10. How did you feel about the true reason behind Muffin's death? Should we fear doing good deeds that may turn out to be the wrong ones?

About the Author

Caroline B. Cooney is the bestselling author of more than ninety suspense, mystery, and romance novels for teenagers, which have sold more than fifteen million copies and are published in several languages. *The Face on the Milk Carton* has sold more than three million copies and was made into a television movie. Her books have won many state library awards and are on many book lists, such as the New York Public Library's annual teen picks. Caroline grew up in Old Greenwich, Connecticut, and spent most of her life on the shoreline of that state but is now in South Carolina near her family. She has three children and four grandchildren. She was a church organist for many years and accompanied the choirs at her children's schools.